RACHAEL'S NEW BEGINNING

JUDITH ABBETT

PublishAmerica
Baltimore

© 2011 by Judith Abbett.
All rights reserved. No part of this book may be reproduced, stored in a retrieval system or transmitted in any form or by any means without the prior written permission of the publishers, except by a reviewer who may quote brief passages in a review to be printed in a newspaper, magazine or journal.

First printing

All characters in this book are fictitious, and any resemblance to real persons, living or dead, is coincidental.

PublishAmerica has allowed this work to remain exactly as the author intended, verbatim, without editorial input.

Hardcover 978-1-4137-4460-6
Softcover 978-1-4626-1098-3
PUBLISHED BY PUBLISHAMERICA, LLLP
www.publishamerica.com
Baltimore

Printed in the United States of America

Rachael's New Beginning is dedicated to my husband David, and my wonderful family; with a special 'thank you' to my friend Martha, for her help and encouragement.

To Wynell from Judy

… So then faith cometh by hearing, and hearing by the word of God.

ROMANS 10:17 KJV

♦ CHAPTER ONE ♦

The sleepy little east coast town in South Carolina was coming to life! A few cars were starting to pull into the parking places in front of the various stores on the main street. Shelly could see some of the doors opening, allowing the clerks and workers to appear, bringing their tables and bins with produce and merchandise outside. Across the street, in the old brick three-story building, the bank sign in the front window was turned from "Closed" to "Open". A few minutes later, an employee came outside to sweep the walk with a huge broom. Within fifteen minutes, the quiet two-lane street had turned into a busy village, with cars, people and noise.

Shelly had been waiting fifteen minutes for one of the offices to open. She had tried the door at nine o'clock, but when no one had answered, she returned to her car to wait. She didn't really mind waiting; it gave her a chance to look over the main street and see the people. After all, she hoped to live here soon! She had chosen this seaside town on the east coast, thinking no one would know her. She could forget the past and have a fresh start. She had prayed, asking God to open doors to a new life, one that would glorify Him.

By nine-thirty no one had approached the office; after checking the door to be sure no one had entered from the rear, Shelly stood on the sidewalk trying to figure out how she should proceed. Remembering the sign for Stan's Café across the street she decided that since she had skipped breakfast at the hotel this morning, she'd see if she could get some tea and toast. Maybe they had a phone book she could check for another realtor. Checking back and forth for traffic, she crossed the main street and entered the café. The interior was a pleasant surprise! It was decorated in a cozy country style, with booths on the right side and tables down the middle of the long room. The kitchen was open to a counter running along the entire length with barstools covered in red leather. Wonderful odors were coming from the kitchen! The fragrance of homemade biscuits and bacon were already making Shelly hungry. Glancing around she noticed a number of folks sitting around with coffee and chatting. The busy waitress motioned her to any booth, so she wandered back to the mid section, looking at the photos on the wall. They were old original black and white photos of the streets and houses in the town. Sliding into a booth, she laid her jacket and purse beside her and looked at the photos on the wall next to her. They showed the café, years ago, with horses and buggies out in the front. The road was packed dirt and she could see tracks from buggies and wagons. A few ladies stood visiting, their long dresses gently blowing in the breeze. The photos were in good condition and Shelly gazed at them thoughtfully. I wonder if they would sell them to me? Probably not, since they're of the café. I wonder if they would let me make copies of them? It might be worthwhile to ask later. Just as she was turning away from the photos, the waitress came over to her table and asked if she wanted coffee.

"Oh! No thank you, I'm not a coffee drinker, but I would love some hot tea and a biscuit," she replied.

"I'll get it." Nodding her head, the waitress put down a set of silverware and napkin and turned away.

"And if it's not too much trouble, may I please look at a phone book?" Shelly inquired.

"What'cha looking for, a realtor?"

"Yes, how did you know?"

"Well, I saw you knocking at Pat's door and you have a newspaper on the table with houses for sale. Here come with me!" The middle aged waitress, whose nametag read "Donna", reached over, picked up Shelly's silverware and newspaper and walked toward the back of the room. Waiting at the side of the back booth, she looked back and said, "Come on, get back here! I have customers waiting." By now, Shelly was bewildered, but she slid out of the red vinyl seat and started towards the back of the row of booths. Motioning her into the booth, the waitress informed her, "You need to talk to him!" Then she turned and walked away!

After sliding over to the middle of the seat, Shelly turned her head toward the rustle of a newspaper being slowly lowered. It stopped abruptly underneath the most beautiful dark gray eyes she had ever noticed! Startled, she started to rise, but the paper lowered more and a deep voice chuckled. "Hello, I see Donna is trying to drum up business for me."

Shelly was so surprised; she just sat there, gazing at the man across the table. He was tall, with dark hair and those beautiful eyes. As her gaze lowered, she was surprised to see a mustache over his firm smiling lips. He was rather handsome, not in a movie star way, but just in an ordinary way. His face was pleasing, and open. Just glancing at him, she thought he was a little older, maybe thirtyish. However, when her glance dropped she found herself staring at a uniform!

"Oh my! I haven't done anything wrong! Why did she bring me here?"

Grinning, the man reached over to shake her hand. "I'm Wade Marsdon. I'm the local Deputy Sheriff and also the 'other' real-estate agent. We noticed you waiting for Pat."

Relieved, she explained, "I had an appointment, but she didn't show up. I was wondering if I could call her."

Smiling, he replied, "She may not have remembered your appointment. Pat's a lovely woman, but I'm wondering if she's not experiencing some kind of age related senility. She seems to be in her own world lately. I'm sorry you had a bad experience with her. She's really a wonderful lady. Maybe there's something I could help you with."

Just then Donna brought more coffee for Wade and some tea for Shelly. "Well… are you just going to sit there grinning Wade? Find out what she wants with a realtor. You need to keep her around." With that, she turned and walked away.

Looking across the table, Shelly asked in a small whisper. "Is that your mother?"

Laughter rang out in the tiny cafe as Wade leaned back in the booth. "Oh that's priceless! No! She's not my mother, but she does tend to think she can meddle in anyone's business! We're so used to her; I don't really notice it any more."

Just then, two heaping plates of bacon and eggs, biscuits, gravy and potatoes were placed in front of them. Donna also put a plate with a stack of pancakes in the middle of the table.

Her protest that she hadn't ordered any food was interrupted by Donna remarking, "Well, I had Stan add to Wade's order since he wouldn't want to be eating in front of you. I figured if you're going to be driving around looking for a place to stay, you'd need to have a good breakfast."

Disconcerted, Shelly thanked her. Gazing at the man across from her, she wondered again if she had made a mistake in coming here. Maybe she'd better look at her map again and find another town where she could work. Timidly she remarked, "I'm not real comfortable with all this."

Probing gray eyes twinkled back at her. "It'll be okay, I promise. Let's eat while it's hot and then we can talk and decide if I can help you. Is that okay?"

"Yes, it'll give me time to think about everything." Seeing Wade start to take a bite, she quickly asked, "Do you say grace before you eat?"

Startled, he nodded toward her, "Go ahead, it's your turn."

When she finished her last bite, Shelly leaned back in her seat. "I haven't had a breakfast like that for years! Those were the fluffiest pancakes I've ever eaten! I wonder what she does to make them so light?"

Wade leaned over and whispered, "She uses buttermilk and carbonated water in them; aren't they wonderful! I never get tired of them! People come from all around to have breakfast here. It's one of the few places that doesn't have greasy food. Now! Tell me what you want? Are you thinking of moving here? At her nod, he continued, "Just you? Do you want to buy a house? Or rent? In town or the country? If you'll tell me what you're looking for and your price range, we can figure out what's available." He reached into his pocket and pulled out a small notebook, flipping it to a fresh page.

Shelly had been watching and thinking about this man sitting across from her. She was leary of telling too much to a stranger, but after all, he was a deputy, obviously well known in town. He was friendly but not at all flirty. She certainly didn't need to get interested in anyone right now, she had the next two years planned out, and she really wanted to stick to her schedule. She would be too busy getting her business going to have time to date. As her realtor, he really did need to know what she was planning, so she could find just the right place. He was also nice… and that meant a lot to her. Maybe having Wade Marsdon help her find a place to live and work was an answer to her prayers.

Leaning back on the cushion, she said, "Well, I'm looking for a place to store furniture, a place to open a shop and a place to live. Three in one would be nice! A house with a barn…maybe a storefront with storage and an apartment on top? Maybe a warehouse with living accommodations in the upper or backspace? I need something visible for selling merchandise." At his quizzical look, she added, "I'm planning to open an antique store a year from now. And right away, I need a place to store and refinish furniture. I would really like…"

Just then, his cell phone rang, and with an "Excuse me", he answered it, grinning at the caller I.D. "Hello Mom… Yes… I don't know… yes, she's very pretty." Glancing at Shelly, he rolled his eyes. "Yes Mom, she's about 5'1" or so. Yes, her hair is brown. Mom… she's sitting right here… She's a client. I don't know. Maybe 115? Blue?"

Shelly was laughing by now and wrote on his tablet; Auburn Hair, Blue eyes. 5' 2" 120 lbs.

"A ring? No Mom, no ring. I don't know. She could be married with six kids."

Shelly wrote; single, no kids, BIG TATTOO!!!. NOSE RING!!!

That brought a huge laugh from Wade and he had to cover the phone. "Oh, you're good!" he chuckled. Back into the phone he said, "Mom, stop! Please listen to me! This is business! Would you be interested in renting out the produce barn?" He grinned as he continued speaking, "I'm not going to tell you, it would be all over town in ten minutes! Well, fifteen. It only took twenty for you to know I was having breakfast with someone. How many calls did you get? What happened to Iris…? Oh, I forgot she's out of town. Mom… Seriously, would you consider it? Ok, we'll be out there in an hour. Would you do a walk through the cabin, and then leave the barn open? Mom… no more! I'll talk to you later. What? Oh, I don't know. No, I'm not going to ask her. I'm sure you'll know by the time we get there. Bye." Looking back at Rachael who was still smiling, he apologized. "I'm so sorry. My mom is the sweetest lady I have ever met, but I still don't understand how she can reduce me to a six year old. As you heard, the phones in this town are well used! No one's malicious; they just don't have enough to talk about. They're curious about newcomers. On the other side- they are the most loving, helpful, considerate folks I have ever lived around. They'll help you in any way they can, and be the first to bring in dinner when you're ill. Just don't tell anyone your business unless you want it known all over," he added with a grin!

"Well then, please don't tell anyone what I want to do! I've been planning on this for a long time, and now that it's working out, I don't want anything to jinx it!"

♦ CHAPTER TWO ♦

Shelly raised her eyebrows as she noticed Wade headed toward his squad car. "This is really going to keep my life private; riding all over in a Sheriffs' car the first day! Could we go in my car?"

"Only if I cut off my legs," Wade replied, with a grin. "It's made for a midget! Come on, folks here are used to my having people in the car. Just smile and you'll be okay."

The next hour was spent driving over the area. Wade pointed out a storefront that was too small, one that was outside the business area. He drove past a couple of moderate homes with garages and two higher priced homes with attached garages. There was also a huge mansion at the edge of town. He mentioned that it was the Addison house, adding the town was named after the family. They walked through a warehouse that needed a lot of work to make it usable and one that was not in a desirable location for a business. Finally, he drove back to the square, and then out of town to the north.

"Our town which was established in 1830 is centered around the original courthouse. There are roads north, south, east, and west from the courthouse, with four cross streets on each, making a grid. Then there are the residential areas to the south and west. This is the north road and this is the last cross road," he pointed out as he passed the side road and turned into a lane that circled back around to the cross road making a semi-circle in front of a huge barn.

"Oh!" whispered Shelly. "This is wonderful! It's so weathered and friendly. It's huge! Look at the parking area and the enormous doors! It would make a wonderful antique shop! Does it have a floor? Is it damp inside? I can't keep furniture in it if it's damp. Is this what you were talking to your mother about?"

"Yes, I saved it for last since I thought you'd want to look at it closely. Shall we get out and look around?" As he watched her, Wade was intrigued by her reaction; she was just glowing with enthusiasm! He had briefly thought she was nice looking while they were in the restaurant, but now that she was so animated, he realized that she was really pretty. She was petite and sweet looking; there was nothing glamorous or flashy about her. She definitely had an outgoing personality; he could tell she liked people. Usually newcomers had friends or relatives in the area, so he wondered why she had chosen their little town to relocate in.

As they walked to the front of the barn, Wade informed her, "This all belongs to my family. Dad farmed and sold produce and hay from our farm and it's already zoned for business. You'd have to check about opening an antique store here, but since I'm on the council, I doubt that it would be a problem. It's really close to town, and with good publicity, it would draw in visitors. It's on the main road to Garden City to the east and we have lots of tourists passing through in the summer. It was used to sell fruits and vegetables, so there's not an animal smell to it, even though there are stalls built along the sides. It also has a small office and a bathroom with running water and it's hooked up for electricity. As to the damp, it has a concrete floor and foundation, with a wood floor on top. It has drains in the floor and we never had any hay mold on us. Dad enclosed the walls with inexpensive wood and the roof's tight."

By then, they had entered into the main area of the barn through the small door on the left side of the big double doors and Shelly was smiling and looking at everything. "Oh, the wooden floor is magnificent! And a counter! How wonderful! This is ideal! Oh, I hope I can afford to rent it! Do you think she'll let me have a business here? Oh, when may I talk to her?" Shelly didn't see the dust and the old farm equipment, she saw in her mind a shop with wonderful antiques everywhere and people browsing around finding little gems, pointing at things saying, 'My grandmother had one of those!' After months of heartache and trauma, she began to glimpse the beginning of her new life.

"Hold on! Calm down! There's more! I'm certain that she'll rent it; actually we'd previously talked about it, but I also know she won't sell any of the property. This will all come to me when she dies, and she won't sell of any of it." Wade hesitated, and then went on. "Maybe I better tell you that Mom, even though she looks good, has cancer. Some days she stays in bed and some days she's able to go out and visit. But the doctors give her... at most... one and a half to two years to live."

Wade seemed to be matter of fact about his mother, and Shelly realized he was covering a hurting heart, but before she could say any thing, he continued telling her about the building.

"So... now then! The barn doesn't have any real accommodations for living in it, but there's a small cabin on down the side road that's for sale. It was just built last year, so everything's new. The owner's moving and has already decided to let it go. I believe with the finances which you have available, that you can buy the cabin, plus rent the barn. You'd be able to walk to work every day. Would you like to look at it?"

"Oh yes! That sounds wonderful! Lead the way."

Wade opened a small door in the back of the barn and led the way over a path, through the trees, along a fence line. The county road was to the right, and on the left were acres and acres of farmland. Soon they came upon a path that led to the front of a small cabin facing the road. It had a picket fenced yard and a wonderful porch all around. Wade opened the lovely oak door and motioned her inside. They entered a large room with a living area on the left side, filled with comfortable chairs and a sofa. The ceiling was high with beams across it, making the room seem extra large. Rachael noticed a small fireplace in the middle of the sidewall, and on the right was a dining table and chairs in front of a small kitchen. Wade took her down the hallway to see two bedrooms with a bathroom between. There was a stackable washer and dryer in a closet off the hallway with another closet for storage next to it. It was compact and just perfect for one or two people!

Looking out the kitchen door Shelly saw a small deck with chairs facing the east. As she turned toward Wade, her face beaming, Shelly sighed. "I love it! I love everything about it! How much land comes with it? Can I afford it? Oh, it's just so sweet! What about the furniture? This would all be so wonderful if it works out. I've prayed and prayed about this and just feel like God is working things out for me. I can't wait to get settled."

Wade had been watching her as she walked around, checking out closets, and cabinets. She had checked the water pressure, flushed the commode and looked under the sink. She was older than he had first thought; she had seemed like a young girl but now he realized she was probably just four or five years younger than he was. She seemed competent and assured. Being in a strange situation at the cafe had thrown her off a little, but now she was back on course. He wondered again why she was here and where she came from. He might just do a background check on her, especially if she was going to do business with his family. Thinking about that, he realized that he didn't even know her name.

"Excuse me Miss," he said in a very formal Groucho way. "I think we need to be introduced. My name is Wade Marsdon. And you are…?"

Expecting her to reciprocate, he was unsettled when she just looked at him.

"Ah… No name? Amnesia…? Trying to think up an alias?"

She held her head to one side in a way that he had noticed before when she was considering an answer, and slowly replied. "I would like to be called Rachael!"

"O…kay…that's a nice name; did you pick it out of a hat?"

"Nooo… it's my name and I'd like to use it! It was my great grandmother's name, and I've always liked it, but no one ever wanted to call me Rachael. I've been known at home and at college and at work as Shelly, and I want to be a Rachael! I don't really care for nicknames, so I think that this is a good time to start being called Rachael. I'll have a new town, a new business, a new house, and a new name! It's a new beginning!"

"Well then Rachael, have you chosen a last name?"

Just then, the phone rang and Wade picked it up. "Wade here," he said, smiling and shaking his head. "Thank you …" as he hung up.

"Mom says there's lemonade in the fridge, would you care for a glass? We can sit outside and talk about finances."

Taking the glasses of lemonade outside, Wade found Rachael leaning on the deck rail, gazing at the fields around the property. Handing her one, he inquired, "Are you interested in this cabin? Do you think it's something that you would like to own? What do you think about all the property we saw today?"

Smiling at him, she replied, "I love the cabin: it's just big enough, with not too much yard to keep up. It's wonderfully designed with lots of little extras and I like the floor plan and the size of it. If I can use the barn, it would be wonderful! But can I afford it? I noticed there's not a 'For Sale' sign in the yard, are you sure the owner wants to sell it?"

"Yes, Rachael, it's definitely for sale! As a matter of fact, it belongs to me. I built it last year before I knew Mom was ill and I've decided to move back into Mom's house, to help her next couple of years. Since I know how little time we have, I'd like to spend more with her. As you probably guessed, she loves to fuss over me! The family house and land will come to me later and I won't need this cabin then. I've already priced the cabin and land reasonably, but you can have the bank officer come out and appraise it if you'd like. If he doesn't think it is worth what I've figured, I'll be willing to adjust the price accordingly. I don't want to take advantage of you, or have you feel like I did. I have a paper at the office where I figured out the price last week, and you can see it and know that I did it before I talked to you. You can also talk to someone else to be sure I showed you everything which is available. I don't want you to think that I'm pushing you into this. But as soon as you mentioned what you were looking for, I knew you'd like this arrangement."

Rachael sat there looking at him. She had prayed before they left the restaurant; then she had prayed as she walked around, and now she had peace that this was her future home.

She felt like God was giving her the desire of her heart! She could see that Wade was frowning; worried that she might think he had done something underhanded.

"Well, I just think that means we'll both be happy! I would love to live here with all the acres of fields around" she commented. Then grinning, she added, "Does that mean the price won't be as much, since there won't be any real-estate fees, and I won't have to pay for an inspection? I'm sure you'll have everything working efficiently. I just need to figure out all the costs and plan how much of an investment it will be."

Rachael had inherited $80,000 from her Nana, and she wanted to put $40,000 down and have enough reserve to pay rent and house payments until her business was stable. It was a plus that the cabin didn't need any remodeling; it was new looking and everything was nice. By the time she had shared her finances, and her projected income, Wade knew she could afford both, but was wondering why she wasn't starting her business for a year. The bank might have a problem about her being unemployed. Actually, he could afford to float the loan for her, but wondered if it was a good decision. When he mentioned the bank would want to know about employment, she hesitated, and then answered.

"Well, you know almost everything else about me; you might as well know what I have planned. Starting next month I'll be employed by a man in Charlotte on a small regular salary and also commission. My job will be to attend auctions and sales around the state, buying large antique furniture for him. He'll have men pick it up and take it to N.Y. or Boston, or wherever he thinks it will sell. Antiques are a big item there and he can make a lot of money, even with paying me and moving it. But… if folks here find out what I'm doing, the prices will go up. That's why I really don't want everyone to know I'm looking for antiques. While I'm looking for his large furniture, I'll be buying smaller things for my shop. I want a cozy, friendly shop where folks can feel free to walk around and look for a long time, finding treasures tucked here and there. I understand that the only other antique store in town is upscale and pricey, so a cozy, rustic barn is just perfect for what I want."

Wade shook his head. "You're a girl on a mission! That seems like a big undertaking for just one person. You seem to know what you want; do you always have everything so organized?"

"Yes, pretty much. I've been planning on this for a long time. Using the barn would be ideal and the cabin would make a cozy home. So if you are willing, I would like to buy the cabin. What do I need to apply for a loan at the bank?"

As he picked up the lemonade glasses, Wade motioned to go inside. "Rachael, it's getting late, I need to be at work in ten minutes. Let's lock up and I'll drop you off in town. I want you to really think about this, and be sure it's what you want to do. It's a big responsibility and I don't want you to feel like I've rushed you into it. Let's meet at nine in the morning at the café and discuss your decision."

Watching Wade rinse and put the glasses in the dishwasher, Rachael asked, "Would you mind if I stayed and looked around for a little while? I promise not to pry into your things. I'd like to be able to remember how the cabin and barn are laid out. The weather's wonderful today; I know I'd enjoy the walk to my car later. It will give me a chance to get the feel of the area."

"Sure, that's fine. Just pull the door closed when you leave and lock the front doors of the barn from the inside and shut the back door. I'll see you in the morning then. Here's a card with my numbers on it if you want to reach me before then."

How wonderful is this! My own little cabin and room for a garden! Rachael walked back through the rooms, planning on furniture she would need. There were no curtains up at the windows, but she would need to have some to give her privacy. The bedrooms had drywall painted white and she wanted to add some color. The living room area was log with white caulking. The kitchen needed a small island; she could look for an old butcher block for the space. When she had closed up the cabin, she walked around the outside and then on to the path taking her to the barn. Approaching the back, she noticed a picnic table and walked over to it. She sat down on the bench and looked around the back of the huge barn. There was a small storage building to one side, but other than that and the picnic table it was cleared off space. Smiling she bowed her head to pray, not realizing that she was being watched.

The lady standing in the shadows inside the barn was also smiling. "*Thank you Lord!*" she whispered. "*She's beautiful and she loves you. You sent just the right wife for Wade. Will you give me the time to see them married and Wade putting You first in his life? Oh! I hope so, it would give me such joy, but if not, I'm ready any time you call me home. Thank you for letting me know about her.*" She quietly stepped back to the front of the barn, giving Rachael privacy. As she stood waiting outside with her golf cart she smiled, thinking about all the changes in the future; for her, for Wade and for the big barn. Within a few minutes, she heard footsteps inside and so she called out, "Hello! Wade said you would be coming back this way."

Startled, Rachael turned toward the voice, but realized immediately who the voice belonged to when she noticed the cart and the lovely older lady standing there. Coming toward her, she held out her hand. "You must be Mrs. Marsdon. I'm Rachael Montgomery."

"Yes Dear, it's so good to meet you. Please call me Rose. Wade says you're interested in buying the cabin? It would make a wonderful place for a young lady... and we would be neighbors! Are you staying in town? I thought you could come to dinner tonight and just stay with me. I have lots of extra bedrooms, and that would give us a chance to get acquainted. You could have all the privacy you want!"

"Why thank you Rose, but I've already made arrangements to stay at 'The Hotel' in town tonight. I wouldn't want to back out on my reservation there. If everything works out, we'll have plenty of time to visit later."

"Yes, Dear, but there's no sense in paying for a room when you can stay at the house. It will save you a considerable amount of money that you can use to personalize your new home! You can just plan on telling Fern in the morning that you're staying with me, and she won't be a bit upset that you're leaving! Just bring your things with you tomorrow and you can stay in one of the upstairs bedrooms, I promise I won't bother you at all. With Wade working nights, I get lonesome for company at meal times, and it would be a blessing to have someone to share a meal."

Oh my! No wonder Wade said she could reduce him to a child. Rachael felt like her life had been taken over and planned without her input. Such a sweet lady, but she sure liked to organize things! The thought came to her though that this might be her landlord and she needed to be especially gracious to her. "Thank you, may I let you know tomorrow? I need to talk to Wade and decide what my next step is. Things are happening very fast, and I don't want to make a mistake."

"I understand Dear, but plan on coming to dinner about five tomorrow no matter what you decide. Wade will be working and we can visit together. If you do decide to buy the cabin, I have some ideas about window treatments. Wade never wanted anything to cover the view, but I'm sure you'll want more privacy than he did. I also have some bedding you may have, and there's surely some furniture you can use stored in the attic."

"My gracious, thank you, but I have my own furniture. I'm just waiting to know where to have it sent. Thank you so much for your kindness! Wade or I will let you know my plans tomorrow. I'm so glad to meet you- now if you'll excuse me, I'll lock up and walk back to my car. I'd like to look around the town."

♦ CHAPTER THREE ♦

Rachael arrived early at the cafe the next morning. She hadn't slept well last night; there were just too many things going through her mind! She had prayed more than once, leaving her feeling peaceful about her plans, but she still felt overwhelmed with how fast everything was falling into place. She was wondering why, when it looked like God was answering her prayers, that she was uneasy because it was happening so smoothly. She knew that God wasn't bound to our time line! She was hardly settled before Donna brought her a lovely teapot and cup.

"Here Rachael, if you're going to eat here regularly, you should have your own teapot. It'll save me from going back and forth so much! Did Wade find you a place to stay yesterday?"

Although she was startled by the abruptness of Donna's statement, Rachael realized that she wasn't being rude, just busy. "Good morning Donna! Thank you for the beautiful teapot! I appreciate having brewed tea; it tastes so much better than just a bag in a cup. Wade's meeting me later, could I have a couple of small pancakes while I wait? They were delicious and I'm hungry today."

As the waitress walked away, Rachael pulled out her list for the bank. She had packed her birth certificate, her social security card, bank accounts and statements in an envelope.

She was going over her estimated monthly output when Wade dropped into the seat across the table.

"Morning."

"Hello Wade! Good morning! You're up early also! I hope you slept better than I did; I had trouble falling asleep; there was just so much to think about! I kept wondering what you had decided about the cabin and barn? I met your mother, but didn't ask her about renting the barn. I thought you might want to talk to her first. Did you have a chance? Will she rent the barn to me?"

"Rachael, wait a minute. I'm sorry, but I'm not a morning person. Let me get some coffee down before I have to be intelligent. I worked late last night and I'm short on sleep."

Just then, Donna placed a huge platter of pancakes on the table with plates and silverware. She returned with Wade's coffee, leaving the pot on the table, remarking. "Let him get a cup down before you even look at him."

Laughing, Rachael reached for her silverware and remarked, "Well then, how about I say grace and you can eat and drink your coffee. I'd hate for you to growl at me." Laughing again at Wade's frown, she asked God to bless the food and to help them make good decisions today.

Wade watched her as she prayed. He was very unsettled today. After he had left Rachael at the barn yesterday, he had driven around the block to come up behind her car. Jotting down her license plate, he ran the number after he had reported in to the Sheriff, Mitch Stone. As the information came up on his computer, the articles listed stunned him.

"Oh man, Mitch look at this." They both read the screen and then Wade linked to other articles. By the time he had finished his search, he was heartsick, and wondered how to proceed.

"Who is this Wade? Someone you know?"

Explaining what had happened at breakfast and the rest of the morning, Wade confided, "Sometimes I think we have too much progress. Computers make it too easy to know too much."

"Well, what're you going to do? Will you still sell her your cabin?"

"Hmm… I've already told her I would. And just because she was accused of these crimes, doesn't mean she did them. The police questioned her and then completely exonerated her. The headlines are shock value to sell papers. The fact that she testified against her brother is puzzling. I wonder if that's why she's here, to forget the past. She looked so happy when she saw the barn and the cabin… I just don't know Mitch. She really didn't do anything wrong, but having her brother in prison is not something I would want the local gossips to know. If she's trying to start over, that sure won't help. The report said that he was spaced out on drugs. I would hate to think she's involved in that in any way. She seems sweet; she prayed for the food and said she had prayed about coming here."

"Huh! That doesn't mean a lot sometimes."

"I know, but I think she's sincere. And beside, she inherited her grandmother's money. If there were anything wrong there, she wouldn't have gotten it."

"Look up the estate and see if you can find out what happened to the brothers part."

After a frustrating fifteen minutes, Wade spoke up. "The grandmother's estate was originally divided into three parts; Rachael, her sister Rhonda and the brother Russell. Because of the assault with a deadly weapon charge, Russell can't inherit; his money was not split between the girls, it was put into a trust by them with the interest going to drug rehabilitation. I also found the obituary; the grandmother died three months after the assault. It looks like Rachael took care of her before she died."

"Well Wade, I don't see that Rachael's done anything wrong. It's unfortunate that her brother's a criminal, but that doesn't make her one. She didn't profit from his share of the inheritance and she's trying to start over. I think you just need to give her the chance she's looking for. We don't get to choose our family members, and some of them aren't law abiding citizens, as you well know." Looking at Wade speculatively, he asked, "Are you interested in her? Is that why you're so upset?"

Sighing, Wade answered slowly. "I don't know. Maybe… she seemed awfully young at first, but then the more I was around her the more mature she seemed. She's intelligent and inquisitive. She has her life planned out for years to come. She also has that sweetness that Mom has, without the chatter," he added chuckling.

"Well, just keep your eyes open, and I wouldn't go too fast. If she was mixed up in the drugs, she may be a user and I'd hate to see you in the middle of that. You know once they start it's a downhill ride."

"Yes, I'm really aware of that. Thanks Mitch, lets just keep this under our hats for now. By the way, will you sign and date this?" he asked, pulling a paper from his IN box. "It just shows that I had decided on the price before I talked to her." Wade mulled over the information about Rachael during the remainder of the day, and tossed and turned for hours before he finally slept that night.

♦♦♦♦♦♦♦

Trying to eat her breakfast, Rachael could sense that Wade was preoccupied this morning. She wondered if it had anything to do with the cabin or barn. She was getting a funny feeling in her stomach and put down her fork.

Watching him, she finally blurted out. "Is something wrong? Have you changed your mind? Not knowing is upsetting me! Please tell me what's bothering you."

Startled, Wade shook his head. "Sorry, I was what my granddad always called woolgathering. If you've decided you want to buy the cabin, it's yours. There's an appraiser out there now, he'll swing by here and let me know what he thinks."

"Wonderful! I'm so glad; I think it will make a wonderful place to live. What about the barn? Did you have a chance to talk to your Mother about it? Did she tell you I met her at the barn yesterday?"

"I talked to Mom at supper last night. I had a chance to go by and grab a quick sandwich while on patrol. She says she'll let you store whatever you want in the barn for now. When you start your business, then you'll have to pay a small rent to her. Until then, you just need to pay the water and electric and your own insurance. But…" He held up his hand to stop her from interrupting. "It comes with some stipulations. First, she wants you to come and stay with her until I can get the cabin ready for you and we get the paper work done. Second, she says you'll have to be the one to clean out the barn and do whatever it needs. I can help with that when I have time, and there are some highschoolers that would love to earn some extra money. Okay…Miss Impatient, it's your turn!"

Leaning on the table, the food forgotten, Rachael shook her head, puzzled. "Why would she let me, a perfect stranger use her barn without payment? And why does she want me to stay with her? It just doesn't make sense."

For the first time, Wade looked a little uneasy, "Well, we might as well get this over with. Mom probably spent yesterday afternoon picking out your wedding dress and deciding what color the others will be." By then his face was flushed and red and he looked extremely embarrassed.

"What? What do you mean? I'm not engaged or... Oh. No...! You mean... She thinks we are...Oh no! Why would she think that? I don't... well, I mean..." Rachael finally came to a stop. She thought Wade was attractive, but she surely wasn't looking for marriage any time soon.

"Rachael I'm so, so sorry, I just thought you should know. Mom wants to see me married and will try her best to make it happen. Nothing would make her happier than to see me married before she dies. This isn't the first time she has gotten ideas. I've had to sit her down and respectfully ask her to stay out of my personal life. I do hope some day to marry, but I'm not in any hurry. I'm not certain that I want to put a family in my life while I'm still a deputy. I didn't mean to embarrass you, but it'll save a lot of confusion and embarrassment later if you know what she's thinking. You couldn't dream up a fiancée could you?" At her negative shake, he went on. "You could stay with her without it being a problem. I told her yesterday you were a client and a neighbor and that was it." His head had been down, still embarrassed, but now he looked at Rachael to see how she was reacting.

She was laughing! Her whole face was smiling and she was laughing! "How did you ever get to be a big strong gun toting deputy and still let your mother intimidate you? That little tiny lady has you quaking in your boots. I can tell you right now, that I'll never ever be afraid of you! You're just a little boy in a big boy uniform."

Sheepishly he nodded, "You have me pegged! Please don't tell the criminals though."

As they were laughing, he noticed Mitch coming out of the bank across the street. Even though he had been talking to Rachael, Wade was aware of who was in the cafe and what was going on in the area. Wade was a very superior deputy, and noticed details that others sometimes missed. He had a degree from the local university, with a major in criminal justice. He also had excelled on the tests required to join law enforcement: the civil service exam, polygraph, physical and psychological testing. After applying for an opening in his hometown area, he studied for his realtor license and spent the extra time building his cabin. Now he worked full time for the department and was available in the morning for the real-estate opportunities.

Mitch entered the cafe and glanced around for Wade. "There you are! Robert asked me to give this to you," he stated as he came to a stop by the booth.

As Wade made room for Mitch in the booth, he introduced him to Rachael and slipped the folded paper from the appraiser into the folder on the table.

"Welcome to our little town, Sweetheart. It'll be nice to have another beautiful lady here in town."

Watching Rachael, Wade saw her nod at Mitch and then busy herself with buttering another piece of toast. But what he also noticed was that with Mitch's rather forward comment; she had toned down her usual friendly smile and glanced down. She definitely did not acknowledge his personal comment or encourage him in any way. It made him wonder if she'd been hurt or had trouble with unwelcome men. She's seemed at ease with me, he realized, but she definitely pegged Mitch for a flirt. It was a shame, because he was really a great guy, but sometimes he was a little too friendly with the ladies. Everyone in town just accepted him as he was, but now Wade realized that with strangers he was too forward and not very sensitive. It was not really a good trait for a sheriff.

Mitch didn't seem to notice anything wrong and after looking openly at Rachael, he turned to Wade. "We have a slight problem. The little nit-wit that was going to do the files decided that she really didn't know computers and couldn't do the transfers. So now, we need to find someone who can tackle this job without messing it up and won't tell the whole town what's in the files. Any suggestions? It has to be done by the end of the month. I can't think of anyone who qualifies that just wants to work a couple of weeks."

As Wade was thinking about this new problem, Rachael spoke up softly. "Is this something I could do? I don't have anything to occupy my time until I move in. I do know computers, although you may think I'm also incompetent."

Wade had to cover his face to hide his grin. He was seeing a new side of Rachael! She wasn't as fragile as he first thought. She sure didn't let anyone walk on her! She might do better than he first thought with a business. She might look young, but he could see now that she was smart and quick and not a bit intimidated by others, even the Sheriff.

Mitch was speaking again, "Well Sweetie, it's just scanning files onto the computer. You have to make an index and correlate everything. It's supposed to take about thirty hours; ten dollars an hour. You could work anytime you want as long as it's done in a month. What do you think Wade?"

"That would be totally up to Rachael. I'm sure she wouldn't have offered if she couldn't handle it."

"Well great Babe, just come on over with Wade later and we'll get you set up." Setting his coffee cup down he started to leave.

"Sheriff Stone? Just a moment please, before you go." Gently but firmly Rachael continued. "I'll do the work for a flat $300.00... and my name is Rachael. It's not Babe, Honey, or Sweetie. If you're not going to show respect to me, then I won't be comfortable working in your office."

"Hey! I don't mean anything, its just talk. Don't get yourself in a snit! I call all the ladies Honey or something friendly."

"It's not friendly; it's too familiar." Smiling, she reiterated, "If you aren't going to speak to me respectfully, I won't help you. It's up to you."

Glancing at Wade who was busily eating his food with his head down trying to keep a straight face, Mitch finally remarked, "Whatever," as he strolled out of the cafe.

With his head still down, Wade whispered, laughing. "Is he gone yet?"

"Just going out the door" replied Rachael grinning. "Sorry if I embarrassed you, but I just don't appreciate strange men being too familiar. Does that mean he doesn't want me to help?"

Wade raised his head and looked at Rachael. "I'm glad you're here, I think you're going to be good for our little town. The women have been complaining about him for years, but no one ever really spoke to him seriously about it. He just laughs me off when I mention it. I feel bad that I didn't say anything today, but frankly, I'm used to him, but when I heard him call you Sweetie, it really got to me! Then when you confronted him, I had to turn away so he wouldn't see me laugh. Hearing a little thing like you intimidate the macho Sheriff made my day! You have a way, little lady, of putting people in their place. Which reminds me, I understand you held your own with my mom yesterday."

Laughing she mused, "I'm not too sure! I'm expected to move in today and be there for dinner at five. Actually, it would be nice to stay there instead of the hotel. Maybe I can help her around the house."

"Great! That would be wonderful! Tomorrow evening is a ladies club meeting at the house. She's missed the last two and they scheduled this month's get together at her house so she could attend. I promised to be sure everything's ready; I've ordered the refreshments from the bakery but knowing Mom, there'll be things you could help her with."

"What kind of a meeting it is?"

Wade laughed and then shook his head. "You'll find out soon enough; I think I'll let Mom introduce you to the ladies and explain it to you."

They spent the next half hour going over the report from the bank appraiser and the contract for the house. The appraiser had put the price higher than Wade was asking, and they discussed the price until Wade finally spoke up. "Rachael, I'm sticking by what I told you yesterday. I think it's sufficient for the cabin. It's a fair price for both of us and I'm satisfied with it. If you're satisfied, then we'll go with that."

Wade had also made a contract for the barn, including all the stipulations that his mother had requested for. He had taken time to type out a list of the bank, utilities and the newspaper. He added the insurance company which he used, with the name of a representative. He put the address of the Chamber of Commerce, and the office where she needed to check about the zoning for the barn. It was when Rachael asked what the bank would need for the loan, that he felt a little uncomfortable. He didn't like knowing her background with out her knowledge, but he knew she wouldn't understand his reason for intruding in her life. As her realtor, he didn't have the authority to pry into her personal life. But as the Deputy Sheriff, he had the right to check into anyone's background that would be living here. "They'll need all of these items you have here. They'll have to call your references and they may ask me to do a background check since you're from out of state."

Rachael looked crushed, but then covered it immediately. His heart just turned over. She looked so vulnerable and fragile and there was also a glimpse of resignation.

"Its nothing to worry about, as long as you haven't been arrested, charged for any crime, or filed bankruptcy. That's all they need to know."

"I've never been arrested, but I hate for anyone to dig into my past. My family has recently gone through some difficult circumstances and I want to start fresh here. I guess the past is always with us. I'll just trust the Lord to work everything out."

Wade's heart went out to her and he impulsively suggested, "Rachael, you know, if you can put enough down that I could pay off my loan on materials, I could carry your loan. I have a good job and don't need the full amount for anything. Having a monthly income would be good security for the future for me. We could set up it with the same interest that the bank is currently charging. What would you think about doing it that way?"

Within a few minutes, they had agreed and Wade left to redo the paper work they needed to sign. They planned to meet at the Sheriff's office when he reported for work at noon. In the mean time, she was going to take her things to his mothers and unpack.

As she drove out of the parking space, she laughed out loud, as she remembered finding a bill under the door of her hotel room this morning. When she went downstairs, she found Fern at the desk, smiling and congratulating her on her new house. "Rose says you'll be staying with her until you move. Isn't she just the sweetest lady! She just loves company and doing for folks. Of course now, she can't do as much as she used too, but she still tries. Up until recently, she was behind most of the events going on here in town. She organized activities to bring visitors coming in the summer and urged the businessmen to spruce up the town to welcome them. Wades' Daddy was a wonderful man too! He was the Mayor you know! We sure miss him around town."

Rachael had done nothing but smile and nod her head. Fern just kept talking as she took Rachael's check and filled out a receipt. Handing it to her, she said, "I included a coupon for a discount dinner for two since you haven't been eating breakfast here. Wade likes to eat here; we have a good dinner menu."

I wonder if all small towns are like this, speculated Rachael. I've met some of the sweetest people, but they sure like to meddle! She had already realized that she needed to be closed mouthed about her business. Moving and starting a new life had been so important to her for the last few months, and now she wanted everything to work out well. She had claimed two Bible verses, the first was a scripture in Romans; 8:28 '...all things work together for good to those that love God' This first verse was the hardest. Sometimes she had to really make herself believe that the shooting of her grandmother and the trial with her brother could ever be used for God's plan. Many times she had to just admit to God that she was choosing to believe that it would eventually prove to be profitable. The second verse was in Psalms 37:4 'Delight thyself also in the LORD; and he shall give thee the desires of thine heart'. The second verse was easier, because since the time she was a little girl when she had prayed and asked Jesus to be her Savior, she had delighted in the Lord. She knew that the peace she had and the feeling of protection she had experienced in the last two years came from God and she was very thankful. Over and over she had experienced answered prayers and knew that God was taking care of her. She had prayed and asked God to allow her to find a new home and a place to start her new business. The only sad part was not being able to share with her grandmother all the blessings. She missed the sharing and times of prayer with her. Maybe in time she would find a friend here which she would have a special bond with.

On her way out of town, she impulsively turned into the lane in front of the barn. They were having a balmy spring day and she opened her door to stand in the parking area, her mind going at full speed. She liked to plan things and have them set in her mind before she started a project. It would irritate her sister, who was more impatient and wanted to get started immediately. Of course, Rhonda had to back up and start over many times, because she didn't have everything she needed or hadn't planned properly. Today Rachael was planning on the landscaping in front of the weathered barn. She would need a sign over the top in place of the one that said "Marsdon Produce." Or maybe she could leave it there and put her sign out by the road and one on the front. The old produce sign looked so authentic above the door and maybe they wouldn't want it taken down. The big double doors were wonderful, but posed a problem. She wanted them open, welcoming anyone to come in, but she couldn't leave them open because of the traffic and dust. Maybe Wade will let me put in other glass doors and still leave the big wooden ones open. She could just visualize pots of flowers to draw the traveler's eyes to the barn and some antique farm implements around the entrance. She might need to put in some gravel so the rain wouldn't keep anyone from parking in front. So much to do! And she was so excited!

Getting back in her car, she continued to the first house past the barn, following the lane to the back of the large three story home. Mrs. Marsdon must have been watching out the window; she opened the door immediately and invited her inside. "Oh, I'm so glad you've decided to stay with me! I get so lonesome. Just bring your things in, and we can have a nice cup of tea and get acquainted." When Rachael entered the cozy kitchen, she noticed that Rose had set the kitchen table with beautiful china for their tea. Rachael recognized the Old Country Roses motif from the Royal Doulton collection and commented on how lovely it was and how special she felt using such beautiful china. "Oh my Dear, I love my china! I have many pieces, and I use it all the time. I decided years ago that I would enjoy it more on the table than stored away. It makes every day special! There's just something about having tea in a nice cup and saucer that makes it delectable. It always cheers me up! My husband started buying it for me as an anniversary gift, and each year he supplemented more pieces. Over the years, family and friends have gifted me with more pieces. One day it will go to Wade's wife; my daughters don't really care for it, so we bought them their own patterns years ago. And if you will notice, Wade uses it when I have it set, but if he comes in alone for something, he uses the Americana that's in the cabinet."

♦ CHAPTER FOUR ♦

After making a quick stop at the post office to change her address, Rachael enjoyed walking to the sheriff's office. That was another thing she liked about this small town! You could park and walk to almost anywhere you wanted to go. Most of the main stores were on the north/south streets, with parking all along the curbs. She noticed how quiet it was as she walked along. There were people and a few cars, but it wouldn't be until April or early May that the town would become busy. She was looking forward to seeing how many visitors came past the barn, and might stop next year.

She had started taking the local paper, and enjoyed reading about all the activities scheduled for the summer. There were fairs and flea markets, swap meets and concerts in the park. She had also noticed an ad for auditions by the Addison Players. They were planning on doing a version of 'Arsenic and Old Lace'. What fun! Maybe later when she was settled, she could be a part of the background workers. They might be interested in borrowing some of her antique furniture for stage props. She made a mental note to ask Wade who to contact about offering her help. She found notices about who had given birth and who had a birthday coming up. This small town paper was certainly different than the big city ones. Those were filled with the negative articles; robberies, murders and catastrophes. Thinking about the difference reminded Rachael of the time when her name had been in the headlines. 'Local shop owner accused of drug dealing.' Having her brother arrested for attempted murder and robbery was bad, but to see her name accused in the paper was devastating! It was a traumatic time for her, but she learned that she had faith enough to trust God for her life. He promised never to leave her or forsake her, and she knew that he had kept His promise.

♦ ♦ ♦ ♦ ♦ ♦ ♦

Entering the Sheriff's office, she was glad to see Wade already there. He introduced her to a nice looking lady named Laurel who took her to a desk in the back of the large room, showing her where to put her jacket and purse. It didn't take but a few minutes to understand what they wanted done with the old files; however Rachael listened closely to what Laurel was saying.

"These are arrest records from years back which need to be put into the computer. The most important thing is that you must never leave files open on the desk, or leave the computer on while you're gone. All of these files are confidential. When you need a break, let me know; if no one extra is in the office, you can just cover everything up and go. Other wise, you'll need to turn off the computer and lock the records back up in the drawer. It's really good that you don't know anyone here, so we won't have to worry about confidentiality as much. If you have any questions, just ask, otherwise I'll just let you get to it."

After setting up the index and contents pages, Rachael had no trouble getting started. The work went fast and soon she was in a smooth routine using the scanner to copy the pages. The noise around her faded into the background and before she knew it, Laurel was standing in front of her, suggesting a break.

"You're a worker! Why don't you finish up your current file, and then take a break. I'll be here and you won't have to close anything down. There'll be people in later on, and you'll need to be very careful."

"Could we turn the desk around so that the screen is facing the back of the room? Then no one could read it? There's room."

"Good idea! I'll get Wade to do it while you're gone."

When she returned to the main office, Rachael noticed her desk had been pulled out from the back wall, and turned around. Now it was much more private to the front area. Getting back in her routine just took a few minutes, and soon it was time to go "home" for dinner. Finishing up the file she was working on, she shut down everything, locked the files away, and gave Laurel the key to the cabinet.

"Good-by! I'll see you sometime tomorrow."

Just as Rachael and Rose were sitting down to dinner, Wade came in the back door. They both started to get up to fix him a bowl of stew, but he waved them down. "Sit, sit, I can get my own bowl, besides, I'm hungry and want a big helping!"

It would have been hard to determine who enjoyed this first meal the most. Rose was thrilled to watch Wade talking and joking with Rachael. She just knew they would be married within the year! And Wade, he probably couldn't have articulated it, but it was nice to have a girl to talk to and share meals with in his home. He wasn't far enough in his thinking to picture her permanently in his kitchen, but he knew it was pleasing. And Rachael? It reminded her of sharing meals with her grandmother, and she was relaxed and charming. She was comfortable around Wade; he was amiable and fun to tease.

The Marsdon home was huge; it had three floors and added on rooms with little reading nooks hidden around the corners of the stairs. Rose and Wade had talked about turning it into a bed and breakfast, but nothing was ever decided. Now however, Rose certainly wasn't up to taking care of paying guests, and Wade definitely didn't have time.

Before he went back to work, they went upstairs to the bedroom Rachael would be using. As Rachael followed Wade to the second floor, she noticed beautiful trim on the stairs and rails. He set her things down, showing her the large attached bathroom. Rachael could tell he loved his home, and thought she would enjoy staying here. It would be a wonderful home to raise children in. Maybe some day Wade would have a wife and children to fill up all the rooms.

Coming back down stairs, she hugged Mrs. Marsdon, "Oh thank you for putting me in the blue room! It's so soothing! I'm sure I'll just feel so comfortable staying there! The furniture in the bedroom is lovely, and the bathroom is exquisite. I love having a claw foot tub!"

"Why, thank you my dear, Wade's sister used that room before she married and moved away; I thought you might like it. It's called the Wedgwood room. You may look over any of the other rooms on that floor or above, you might find one you like better. The only one being used now is Wade's old room, but he'll be moving his things out of there soon."

"This one's perfect, thank you so much for letting me stay here. I'm anxious to get into my own home though! It's hard to be patient! Wade mentioned there were some things he needed to do before he moved his things out."

"I think he's planning on moving into the first floor rooms here. He thought it would bother me for him to be going in and out at all hours if he were upstairs. There's another bedroom and bath on this floor he's going to use. My rooms are in the front on the left. We combined the two rooms and made a bedroom with a bath and closet for me. I just cannot get up stairs very well anymore. On days I have to use a wheelchair, I can get around down here pretty well. So, Wade's going to move out the things in the downstairs room so he can put in his things from the cabin. I don't know what we'll do with all the extras; I'm hoping you can use some of the furniture. Some of the things will just look lovely in your new place, I've been thinking about the things you'll need."

"Thank you, you're so thoughtful, but I do have things coming. My grandmother left me all her home furnishing, plus I have furniture and antiques from our shop. As a matter of fact, I need to know when Wade will be out so I can let the movers know when to bring my things. I also need to get the barn cleaned up before then, because I have a moving van full of things to store."

"I'm sure Wade will be busy on Monday, getting the rooms here changed, and his things sorted and moved over. Then Tuesday the cleaning lady is coming to do the carpets and windows and just polish up the cabin. I told Wade that he needed to finish up a couple of little projects he's started over there. It certainly won't do for him to leave anything unfinished! You can just stay here until you get things ready!"

"You're so thoughtful Rose, but I don't mind doing the cleaning. I have some things I want to do before I move in, but I don't want to impose on you any longer than necessary. Since I have nothing to do the rest of the evening, is there anything I can do to the bedrooms or to get ready for the party tomorrow?"

The remainder of the evening, Rose stayed in her wheelchair, instructing Rachael as she rearranged the two bedrooms. She took down the flowered drapes in the bedroom that Wade was moving into. She stripped the bed and replaced the flowered pattern with a nice plaid spread and matching drapes, even though Wade would be moving some of the larger furniture soon. One dresser contained linens and she arranged them in other places where Rose wanted them. Rose employed a housekeeper that came three days a week, so the house was sparkling clean, but Rose needed someone to do all the little extras she wanted done. When they finished in the bed room, she put the finishing touches on the serving table, adding the flower arrangement in the middle.

The next morning she cleaned up the breakfast dishes for all of them, and then walked to the office. She thought it would be better for her to be out of the way while Wade was there moving things around. On entering the large office, she introduced herself to another lady who was at the desk, who returned her greeting with a smile.

"Oh hello! Mitch told me you might be around this week; it's so good to meet you. My name is Mary; if you need anything just let me know."

Rachael was soon involved in her work, but was aware of noise in the room from time to time. Sheriff Stone came in with a man in handcuffs, nodding as he passed her desk on the way to a back room. Mary picked up lunch from the cafe, and they shared it at Rachael's desk at noon. Mary was closer to her age, and they really enjoyed talking to each other. She shared information about the town and the people living there, and also invited Rachael to church, but Rachael answered that she would be going with Rose.

"Great! That's the church I attend also. It's a wonderful church; there's a sweet spirit in the people. The other churches in town are nice, but I attend there because they truly preach the Bible. Everything is based on the Word of God, and the

Pastor's wonderful! We also have a young adult class if you'd be interested; Rose can tell you where to go."

"Does Wade go to church at all?"

"No, not since he moved out to go to college. He always had some excuse, and believe me all the girls in the unmarried and the college and career class tried to get him to come. However…" she leaned down to whisper gleefully in Rachael's ear, "He has never dated anyone since he returned! Having breakfast with you was a milestone in his life!"

♦♦♦♦♦♦♦

After a quick bowl of chowder, Wade, Rose, and Rachael straightened up the kitchen, making sure everything was set for the ladies meeting. Wade answered the door and introduced Rachael as she took the coats from the visitors.

Soon they were all gathered in the sitting room and Rose called Rachael to come in so she could introduce the ladies. "Rachael this is our ladies group! Our mothers were friends during the war, and went through a terrible time trying to continue a sheltered, secure home life while their husbands were gone. Everything was so dreary; they tried to brighten up the town. They started a garden club, and the only thing that didn't change during that time, were the beautiful flowers. In times of sorrow, despair and hunger, learning to cope with all that came with the war, they saved and planted bulbs; cut and started flower bushes and fruit trees. While the men were gone, it was the promise that beauty would again come to our town, that the world was still going on and they could see the blessing God had for them. It helped the ladies keep a positive attitude, and when the war was over, and the men came home, those ladies in the garden club named their daughters after the flowers." Rose gently smiled at Rachael who was standing silent with a look of wonder on her face.

"So… with that said, let me introduce to you Fern, who runs the Hotel. Iris is our baker. I believe you met Laurel at the station, and also Mary- Marigold to us! The lady in yellow is Daisy and Violet is sitting next to her. Jasmine and Calla are on the loveseat. Myrtle's out of town, and we have lost the others. Some have moved out of town, some have passed away, but we still try to keep the club going. We do have some second-generation blooms among us, and we are open to anyone who would enjoy helping beautify our little town. So, this is our flower garden! What do you think?"

Just then, Wade entered the door behind Rachael and leaning over her shoulder with his hand on her arm, he teased, "Don't kid yourself, Rachael they call themselves the flower garden, but locally they are known as the 'Blooming Idiots'…!"

"Oh Wade!" Horrified Rachael turned around to him, "How can you say that?"

Laughing, he said, "Oh it's a term of affection, we love every one of them." The ladies were laughing also, and Jasmine spoke up. "Yes, we use that as the name for our booth at the fair and everyone stops to see what we're selling."

"Oh! What a relief! Wade! That wasn't nice!"

"Yeah, I know, but it sure is fun! I don't get to do it very often. Everyone around here knows them. Besides it's the only way I can get back at Mom; if I had been a girl she was going to name me Pansy.!" Rachael could tell the ladies enjoyed the teasing and realized that Wade was well liked and respected.

Just then, Wade's cell phone went off, and he excused himself. Soon he motioned Rachael into the kitchen. "I have to go in. I probably won't be home until three or four in the morning. Would you turn the coffee on, and serve the ladies. Don't let Mom do anything; I saw her take a pain pill earlier and she won't be steady on her feet. As soon as everyone leaves, get her to go to bed; I'll help clean up in the morning. Thanks Rachael, I'm glad you're here." He had been unbuttoning his shirt as they walked down the hall, and now he disappeared into his room. Within just a couple of minutes, he appeared again in uniform holding his gun, hat and a jacket. Checking for his cell phone and keys, he was out the door and in his car before she could even say anything to him. The rest of the evening was nice, but the ladies could see that Rose was tired, and they didn't stay long. Rachael served the refreshments and took care of all the hostess duties, leaving Rose to enjoy the chatter and gossip with the ladies. Remembering Wade's suggestion, she cleaned as she went, and by the time the ladies had gone, most everything was in the sink soaking. Rose had used her Old Country Roses tea set, and Rachael was very careful handling it. She washed the dishes by hand, enjoying looking at the artwork on the china, and soon had most everything straightened up in the kitchen. Waving goodbye to the ladies, she ushered Rose into her bedroom and conveyed Wades' wishes. "You're to go straight to bed! No chatting or cleaning up! I have almost everything washed, and it won't take me a minute to finish. We can visit in the morning." Seeing her start to protest, Rachael leaned over, hugging her. "Thank you for letting me come here. It's such a blessing, please let me help you."

After she put the last dish away, Rachael fixed a plate of sandwiches and cake for Wade. She decided he wouldn't want coffee in the middle of the night, so she made some cocoa and put it in a thermos, setting it on the table where he would see it immediately when he returned. She also left a note saying Rose was fine, and they were going to church in the morning.

Finishing up her kitchen work, she walked around the house, checking the doors, noticing the beautiful antiques in the various rooms. Wade was the third generation to live in the house, and it held furniture and pictures from past years. Everything was elegant and shone with years of polishing and love. Rose had some wonderful antiques and Rachael spent a long time just enjoying gazing at them in a home setting, wondering where they came from and the stories behind their being used to fill a house with love. What stories they could tell, memories of past sorrows and loves. She hoped that Rose would have the time to share about her ancestors.

♦ CHAPTER FIVE ♦

Sunday was a glorious day: the sun was shining, the temperature was in the high fifties, and the feel of spring was in the air. It was the first Sunday in March, and soon it would be time for the early flowers to start coming up. Rachael had seen the stalks of daffodils and what might be some crocus by the driveway. She felt sure that there would be numerous flowers in the yard as soon as it warmed up more. The days had been sunny and so the temperatures in the fifties and low sixties had not bothered her.

Driving up to the church, Rose directed Rachael to drive under the awning where they could see a young teenager waiting with a wheelchair. After he opened her door, he greeted Rose by name and helped her into the wheelchair, being very careful with her Bible bag and purse. Rachael parked along the lane, and then gathered her things together before walking back to the entrance to the church. As she entered the lobby, she spotted Rose talking to a group of ladies and as she walked over to them, she recognized some of the ladies from the Garden club… the 'Blooming Idiots', she remembered with a smile.

"Hello my dear. Rachael, these are my precious friends. You've met some previously, but this is Rhoda and her daughter Ivy."

It was a blessing to see how much Rose was liked by the ladies; she was certainly gracious and pleasant to be around. Her illness may have attacked her mobility, but not her disposition. She had a sweet spirit and a smiling face. Everyone could see the inner joy that nothing could take away.

In a few minutes, Mary came up to take her to the young adult Sunday School room. There were about twenty-five men and women filling the seats, chatting or opening their Bibles. After choosing a seat in the center of the back row, she glanced around the room, noticing that Ivy and Mary were there along with another young lady that had been standing with the group around Rose. The teacher was a middle-aged man with a smiling face and twinklie eyes. After greeting the visitors and regular members, he began the lesson by asking them to turn in their Bible to the last chapter of Ezekiel. He was so enthusiastic! After reading the first section, he told the class, "This is a difficult chapter, it tells us of the return, the reign of the Lord. It's not the rapture; it's not dealing with the seven year tribulation, but what follows after. This scripture records the Battle of Armageddon and the return of Jesus to the land. The first time He comes, only the saved will see Him and we'll all go up to meet Him in the air. Then comes the seven years of tribulation here on earth. During the end of the tribulation, many nations will be at war against the nation of Israel. Just as the enemies are gaining ground, Jesus will return to the Mount of Olives where He promised He would come and then He takes up the fight for the Jewish nation. Everyone will see Him as He plants his feet on the Mount of Olives. Many people think this is a fairy tale, but it comes straight from the Bible, which is God's infallible word. We can believe these scriptures just as we can everything else that is recorded in the Bible."

Rachael was enthralled with the lesson, realizing that she had not really studied this portion and didn't know much more than the basics of the Lord's return. The teacher went on to tell them that Jesus would rule over the world and set up his kingdom on earth. Rachael was totally concentrating on what Mr. Easton was saying when he threw up his fist and proclaimed that this was the culmination of all the scriptures; that Jesus would come again and rule the earth and every one would worship Him! The class all clapped and said "AMEN!" Just then, a bell rang and Rachael let out her breath. She hadn't realized that she had been holding it until her concentration was distracted. What a lesson! God will do just as He promised!

Following the class out of the room and down the hall to the sanctuary, Rachael was thrilled to have heard about the Lord today and thanked Him for allowing her to hear the teacher. When she found Rose at the end of the aisle on the right side, she slipped in beside her. "Oh! Thank you for asking me to this church, the lesson was wonderful! I need to get my books here so I can study the passage Mr. Easton taught on. He's a wonderful teacher, and I really want to find out more about the Lord's return."

After church Rachael brought the car up to the door and the same young boy helped Rose into the front seat. They had planned to meet Wade at twelve fifteen at the cafe, but Rose mentioned that she was really weary after last night and this morning and that she would rather go home. "Wade will be waiting for us, so I think you should just let me out at home and then go back and have lunch with him!"

Entering the cafe, Rachael spotted Wade in his favorite seat in the rear with his back to the wall. He had told her it gave him opportunity to keep an eye on what was happening in the room. Sliding into the seat, she smiled, and said, "I think we've been set up."

Wade just shook his head, "I guess Mom decided that she was too tired to have lunch today?"

"Yes, she asked me to take her home, but I have a feeling that she could have come if she wanted to! She actually was really animated this morning. I think she gets lonesome at home and enjoys visiting with her friends at church. But she thought having lunch would be too much today."

"Well don't say I didn't warn you that she's a matchmaker along with half the other women in this town! So let's just enjoy lunch together; the roast beef is wonderful, and so are the lasagna and the meatloaf."

Rachael realized that he was somewhat embarrassed, but was trying not to make a big thing about it, so she tried to bring up subjects that were impersonal. They talked about the job at the office and the work planned for tomorrow. Wade had told her she could start painting anytime she wanted. He would be doing some wiring and putting up some crown molding around the cabinets and it would not interfere with the bedrooms. He also had planned to hook up the garbage disposal and would be doing some plumbing in the bathroom. He had put in a whirlpool tub and it needed some work. Since he usually showered, he had not gotten around to finishing it up. He had installed it because of an old football injury that sometimes gave him trouble when he had been working a long time at a stretch.

Soon lunch was over and they headed home in their separate cars. Just as they were approaching the barn, Rachael heard a honk and saw Wade's turn signal come on and so she followed him into the driveway. He wanted her to take a look around the barn with him, so picking up her jacket, she followed him into the dark interior of the old barn.

"Rachael, listen, Mom doesn't want anything that's in the barn; and I don't want much either. We're not farming any longer and we just don't need the old tools and implements we needed before. She wanted to know if you want the things that have been left, thinking you could sell them when you get your shop open. She said it would be better to give them to you than to pay someone to haul it away. But if you don't want to mess with it, I'll call someone and get it cleared out as soon as possible."

Looking around Rachael mused, "Wade there are wonderful things here! Just looking around I can see at least $2,000 — $2,500 worth of farm things. Certainly, I can sell them, but only if I give her the money."

"I told her you would say that. How about fifty-fifty? You do the work and I won't have to mess with any of it?" he suggested grinning.

"Sure, but I'll need help to get it all moved into a pile so I can clean the stalls and beams. Then I'll want to put it into some of the stalls until I can clean everything up."

"Okay it's a deal! I have boys coming tomorrow, it's a school holiday. I'll sort out what I want to keep, and then they can move anything you want where ever your little heart desires!"

Just then, Rachael's cell phone sent out a buzz startling her. She turned towards her purse which she had dropped onto the counter in the middle of the huge barn. "I wonder who's calling me on my cell phone? Very few people have my number." Looking at the ID, she grinned and then answered. "Rachael Montgomery. Yes, well… it's me… I'm not using my nickname any more… I'm sorry Mr. Anderson; I couldn't possibly help you out. If you'll remember, my contract starts on the twentieth. I'm in the middle of acquiring a place to live and work. I also need to check out vans. ... Yes, I've found a place to store things, but not until the weekend."

Rachael was still grinning as they walked around the barn with Wade moving things around so they could see what was in the stalls. "Yes I understand, if that's your proposition I expect to be compensated double until I go on full time payroll. I also expect you to provide a truck and have the account set up at the bank before two o'clock on Friday... Well then, you'll have to find someone else to go to the auction. I informed you at the very onset that I would never use my own money to purchase anything for your business. I don't have the funds to do so and it's too confusing to keep accounts. You worked with my grandmother for years, and I hope we can work together, but if you can't keep your word, then we can void the contract... that will be fine. I'll expect them by two on Friday." Closing her phone Rachael grinned at Wade. "Well, I was planning on going to the auction on Saturday and now I may have the fun of purchasing something."

"You sure put him through the wringer. I take it you're trying to keep the upper hand?"

"You're very perceptive. Yes! Actually that's the reason I was so outspoken. I just knew he would want me to do this and I don't want him to start taking me for granted. He worked with my grandmother for years, but somehow I just don't trust him. The set up he's giving me to shop for him is really a blessing. It'll give me a chance to purchase things for my shop, while earning a living this coming year. He's... just... I don't know, not pushy exactly, but rather narrow-minded. He's interested in his business no matter how it inconveniences his employees. When my Nana died, he told me she had sold him some things in the shop, but he couldn't come up with any bill of sale, and there were no sales recorded in our accounting. I'd been running the shop for eight months and I would've known if anything had been sold to him. I guess he thought I didn't understand the accounts and was too young to stand up against him. But I knew he was trying to put one over on me and I just wasn't having it! I don't want him to get the upper hand. We'll see if he gets the van and the finances here in time."

Wade had his uniform on and was trying to keep clean, but he was interested in seeing what was in the old barn. It was dusty and filled with odds and ends. One whole stall was filled with wooden fruit trays and bushel baskets. After glancing around he decided that there wasn't anything he couldn't live without and told Rachael to do whatever she wanted with it all. By then it was almost one o'clock and he needed to show up at work in a few minutes. They locked up and Rachael drove on to the house to see how Rose was and if she needed anything.

♦ ♦ ♦ ♦ ♦ ♦ ♦

With the walls in the largest bedroom already painted and the trim started on the third, Rachael was satisfied with her choice of color. It was a dusky washed denim blue, soft and soothing. She had finished the bathroom by mid-morning and now was busy working on the bedroom when Wade's voice startled her from the doorway. "Wow! So much for white walls! I didn't even think about real color on the walls, I guess I thought you were going to do something like beige or cream. It sure looks different!"

"Oh Wade, does it bother you? I didn't think about how you would feel about someone changing what you've done. You spent so much of yourself building the cabin; it must make you sad to see it changed."

"No… Rachael, really it's okay. I don't feel bad about your paint choice. As a matter of fact, I think it looks nice. It's restful and rather homey." Today he was dressed in work clothes, jeans and a sweatshirt, so he leaned over, grabbed the roller and started painting the last wall. "I did enjoy building the cabin. I was waiting for the job to open up as deputy and was studying for my realtor license. Coming here was restful and helped reduce stress. Mom and Dad were glad to have me live with them, but I wanted my own place. I had a sense of accomplishment when I finished it, but it never felt like home somehow. With my hours, I'm not here much anyway. I hope you can settle in and make it your home, not just a house."

Rachael had continued to trim the wall while they were talking, but now she put her brush down and turned to Wade. "I think I know why it was never 'home' to you. You've grown up in a house that is filled with generations of family. There are pictures on the walls and the rooms are filled with furniture and mementoes of your ancestors. It's comfortable and roomy and you have wonderful memories there. This place, although you built it, has no memories, and is not full of life yet. Your furnishings are just basic, functional, but you don't have memories anywhere. I didn't notice any personal things anyplace. A house needs love to make it a home and you just haven't gotten that far yet. You've not had anyone to share it with."

Wade had listened and realized that she was spot on with her analysis, but he also realized that she had not said one of the important things. "What about you? You'll be living here alone also. How will you get the feeling of home and love here?"

"All the things I have will be on the trucks coming on Friday and next Wednesday. I have all my grandmothers' things from the house and the shop. I can choose whatever I want to fill the rooms up with memories and family pictures. Hopefully by this time next month, it will look as though I have lived here for years. I plan to make it my little nest, away from all the pressures of the world and stress of my job. But most of all, it will be filled with my Bible and study books. I'll have wonderful Christian music playing and everything in the house will glorify God. Hopefully it will be His love that people feel when they visit."

Laying down the roller Wade stood and smiled at her. "I'm sure if anyone can do it, it will be you." Just then they heard a noise outside in the yard, and Wade looked out the window, remarking, "Well, I came over to talk to you about what you wanted the boys to leave in the house, so I guess we'd better take a break from painting and discuss it."

He had told Rachael that he had everything out of the cabin that he wanted, and that she could have anything that was left. What ever she didn't want, he was donating to a family in town who had been burned out of their house. A fire had gutted the main house and everything was gone. They were in the process of rebuilding the main part of the house, but for now were living in the garage. Others were donating and by the time they moved back in the house, they would probably have more than enough to furnish it.

They did a quick walk through the cabin with Rachael choosing a rug and a small table. She decided on keeping the small gas grill on the deck and the porch furniture. There was also a small storage building in the back with a lawn mower and the tools she would need to keep the yard work done nicely. By then, the boys had finished with their soft drinks and they packed up all the kitchenware and the furniture, placing it in Wade's truck to take into town. While Wade was finishing the plumbing and electrical work, Rachael moved her paint things into the other bedroom. She started on the walls, and was almost finished with the lower portion when Rose called out to them.

"Hello! Is anyone home? I've brought lunch for the tired and weary!" Following the voices into the bedroom, she stopped at the doorway. "Oh, Rachael, it's beautiful! What a wonderful shade of blue you've chosen! Look how the light plays on it! It will be so restful at night with the lower lights. You can just put little curtains up and add a little table over here. A rocker in this corner would be wonderful! There's one in the attic that you may have! Wade can bring it over after lunch. I have just the bedspread to put in here also. It will match perfectly with your color, and be just wonderful."

Wade and Rachael glanced at each other, realizing they were both thinking the same thing: that Rose would have everything just as she wanted it, unless Rachael stood firm.

Ignoring his teasing look, Rachael hugged Rose and turned her towards the kitchen. "Wonderful, my first meal in my new home, with two of my favorite people! What a wonderfully thoughtful woman you are to think about our lunch. We'll just clean up a little and be right with you."

When Rachael returned from the bathroom, Rose had cleaned the counter, and placed paper plates and plastic forks on the napkins. Wade was pouring drinks and had brought in three chairs from the porch. It was nice outside but too breezy to sit out and eat. They enjoyed the food and relaxed after working so steady all morning. However as soon as they finished, Rachael started cleaning up the food. She wanted to get the painting done and go to the office to work on the files this afternoon, and it was already twelve-thirty. By one-thirty, she was finished and just putting away the tarp and paint cans when Wade stuck his head in the side door.

"Rachael? Can you come to the barn a minute? I need to know what you want done with all this stuff laying around. The boys are back from lunch and ready to work again."

Looking around at the piles of old machinery and accumulation from over the years, Rachael felt rather overwhelmed, but knowing that it would only get done by doing one thing at a time, she decided to have everything moved to the center so she could clean the stalls and rafters. Wade had the boys move everything out and then he brought in a power washer. "We used this after every season, trying to get the fruit and vegetable juice out of the barn. The floor's not tight, so it will let the water drain and run off. It's not loose enough to let in mice, but you probably should get a cat once you open up. It also would be a good idea for you to get a dog to guard the house at night, since you're all alone out here."

♦ CHAPTER SIX ♦

It was after two o'clock when she finally arrived at the office, waving at Mary as she passed her desk. By six, she had completed the last file and finished up all the work Mitch had asked her to do. Even though she had been very meticulous, it had only taken her sixteen hours. She was efficient and kept working without breaks and chatting to the other people in the office. In all, it had been very interesting, until she realized that she recognized some of the names. When she started on the 'S' file, she typed in Robert Stevens and it wasn't until she read the age that she realized it was Bobby that had been at the barn this morning. His court records were sealed, but the sheriff's record showed he had been picked up for leaving the scene of an accident and being under the influence of drugs. This was the first sealed document she had come across and she wasn't sure what to do since no one had mentioned it when they gave her instructions, so she made a note on a separate page with the information stating there was a closed file in the paper folder. Surprisingly the next name popped out also. It was Randy Stone age sixteen, the sheriff's son! He too had been at the barn today and Rachael wondered if there was a connection. His records were also sealed, but the arresting report indicated that he had been under the influence of drugs and had run his car into a fence. She could see why the sheriff would be concerned about having just anyone reading these files. He probably didn't realize she had met the boys so soon after moving to town. After reading the two files, she bowed her head and prayed for them by name, asking God to put a shield around them to keep them from the evil of drugs. She'd had such a traumatic time with her brother; she knew first hand what drugs could do. The influence of drugs could cause anyone to do things they would never believe they could do. In her mind, she could still see her grandmother lying on the floor after being shot. She still pictured the blood running down from her leg and making a puddle on the oriental carpet. Just remembering caused her to shiver, and she had to make herself continue her work.

By Thursday evening, she was exhausted. Along with finishing the computer files, she had finished the painting, cleaned the kitchen cabinets and appliances. The carpet cleaners had been there and after the bedroom carpets had dried, she had vacuumed and washed all the windows. She scrubbed the bathroom and the laundry area, and then decided that she would pressure wash the deck that went all around the cabin. There were a few slight scratches on the hardwood floors in the living room, and she touched those up with sealer Wade had left in the laundry cabinet.

Next she started on the barn. Wade and the boys had moved everything in to the center and washed the walls and floors. She sorted the remaining stacks and piles of farming utensils and implements. There were canning jars and buckets, old shovels and rakes. She found farm implements which she didn't recognize and wondered what their function was. She would have to look them up on the Internet. She sure didn't want to ask Wade and have him know how ignorant she was about farming! By the time she had cleaned off what she would keep and put the rest in a pile outside, her muscles were complaining with each move. Rose finally came in her golf cart to persuade her to stop and rest before she became ill from all the dust.Rachael hadn't realized it was so late, she had been thinking about her life while she worked and the time had flown by. She was still deciding which stalls to put her grandmother's things in and which things she wanted taken to her new house. But she was also thinking about Wade. She really liked him! He had been such a help and had unselfishly taken his morning time and his day off to help her. She had watched him interact with the boys who had come to help, and realized that maybe they didn't want to be there but that they were working out the community service they had been sentenced. They had not been particularly courteous to her, mainly ignoring her and talking to each other until an adult came close. Wade treated them as adults, with respect but a firm voice of authority that left no doubt that he was in charge. She had a lot of respect for his interaction with them. He also was friendly with her, but had never overstepped just a friendly relationship. She had planned out her next few years, and had not even considered that God might bring her a husband, but now she wondered. She realized that she liked being around Wade; she enjoyed his humor and his friendly teasing. One day when the sun was shining in the door, he had stood in the light and she had noticed that there was a small scar on his face from the middle of his cheek to the corner of his mouth. It was hidden mainly by his bushy mustache, but she noticed that there was a little pucker on his lip. She had not asked how he had received the injury, but assumed it came through his job at the sheriff's office. Smiling, she realized that it didn't bother her; it just made his face more interesting. As she continued to sort and move things in the old barn, she prayed for Wade. She knew that there could never be any more to their future unless he realized that he needed a relationship with Jesus. Startled, she paused, and pondered her prayer. *Lord? Was my motive wrong? I'm so sorry. I want to see Wade saved because he needs to realize your love, not because of me. If anything ever comes of our friendship, it will have to be based on your foundation, but he needs to trust in You no matter what happens between us. I know Rose has been praying for him all his life, and probably others are also. Will you help me to have insight to share your love with him? Thank you Lord, in Jesus name, Amen.*

In the middle of the night Thursday, Rachael woke up from a restless sleep, sore and thirsty. She had been tossing and turning for over an hour, and just couldn't refrain from thinking of all the little things she needed to do before the moving van arrived in the morning. She drew on her robe and went in search of aspirin and something to drink. Looking over her options, she chose some orange juice and curled up in the love seat in the breakfast nook as she drank it. Just as she finished and was putting her glass in the sink, she heard the back door open, and Wade entered the kitchen. Startled, she turned toward him, and he stopped, looking at her in surprise.

"Well, hello. What are you doing up at three in the morning?"

"I needed some aspirin. What are you doing sneaking home at three in the morning, young man!" she teased accusingly. "You've been putting in long hours at work besides what you've been doing at home. Would you like something to eat or drink?"

"Yes, and I'm bushed. What are you drinking? Orange juice is fine. We had a wreck out on the highway south of town. We're short handed right now; one of our men had to take off work today. His wife has cancer and he wanted to go with her to the hospital in the city, so I had to stay and cover the accident. The cars were messed up pretty bad, but the people will all be okay. It just takes time to process everything and make reports."

Watching him as he leaned against the counter, Rachael realized that he was beginning to be very special to her. She worried about his safety when he left the house, and prayed for him every morning along with his mother. This won't do, she thought! It just won't do!

"I think I'll try to get to sleep; the movers will be here sometime between ten and noon. See you sometime tomorrow!"

She left rather abruptly, because all of a sudden she had felt somewhat uncomfortable standing in the kitchen at three in the morning in her robe. Climbing in beneath the handmade quilt that Rose had put on her bed, Rachael started quoting scriptures; it was the best way she knew to clear her mind of stress and fall asleep.

She was just buttering her toast the next morning when she heard someone in the other room. Reaching over, she turned the coffee pot on, and then took her toast and tea to the table. When she heard footsteps coming through the door she smiled, but it turned to surprise when she saw Wade and not Rose entering the kitchen! Glancing at her, he put in some toast and stood waiting for the coffee to finish. He was a mess! His hair was sticking up in the back and he had on old clothes. His eyes were red and it didn't look as though he had slept at all. It was all she could do to keep reading her Bible and not laugh out loud.

Finally pouring a cup of coffee, he sat down across from her. As she had guessed, he hadn't slept much last night. He kept remembering how nice it was to come home and find someone there to talk to. Then he had to be honest with himself, it was having Rachael there that he liked! He was going to miss her when she moved to the cabin. He had enjoyed having meals with her and playing Scrabble in the evening when he was off from work, kidding her when she made up words. They had spent time working in the cabin and barn together and he had really felt comfortable working with her. He liked being with her; she was fun to tease. But since he wasn't looking for a serious relationship, maybe he didn't need to spend so much time with her. He had finally drifted off to a restless sleep after deciding he wouldn't be around her as much once she moved. That would be the safest thing to do…maybe not the best, but the safest.

Rachael waited until he had drunk most of his coffee and then smiled and said, "Good morning Wade! I didn't expect to see you up so early today. You didn't get much sleep last night."

"I'm off today! Chris came in, so Mitch told me to stay home. Have you been in the office in the barn? When she shook her head, he continued, "I forgot all about it. It probably needs to be emptied out before you put your things in. The desk and file cabinet are full of records and papers. I thought I'd get it cleared out for you this morning."

"I forgot all about it too! I cleaned the bathroom and put supplies in there, but I didn't even think about the office, it's kind of hidden in the back. But Wade, you don't have to do that today. I'm sure you have other things you need to do on your day off. You've helped me so much already! I can just move things in a corner and you can get to it on a rainy day."

"Actually I'd rather get it done. I don't like to have things unfinished. Do you want the refrigerator left in there? And how about the desk and file cabinets?"

"Yes to all, if the refrigerator still works. I guess I'll put my computer in there and keep the records of the business on it. I have about two hours or so until the movers come, so I can help pack up the paperwork and get it swept. I'm finished here, I'll get started." Closing her Bible, she cleared her dishes and poured Wade another cup of coffee.

"I checked on your mother, she's reading in bed and said she'd be up later. When I was out yesterday, I bought cold cuts and chips for lunch today. She's planning on bringing it over later if she's up to it. See you soon."

Just to open the huge barn brought such joy to Rachael! As she stood in the middle of the sunshine from the doors, she thanked God for his protection and provision over her. As she proceeded to the small office in the rear of the barn, she sang one of her favorite hymns and just enjoyed being alive as a child of God. She plugged in the refrigerator and started taking old calendars and lists off the walls and within a little while, she was ready to clean and move the furniture around the way she wanted it.

Wade had entered the barn, and when he heard Rachael's wonderful alto voice, he stopped and listened. Although he had gone to church as a child; actually until he left for college, he hadn't heard the old gospel songs for years. As he listened, the words cut deep in his heart. 'Have you any room for Jesus? He who bore your load of sin'… Time for business and for pleasure… Sinner won't you let him in?' Shaking his head, he started whistling the melody and stuck his head in the doorway. "Hey there, pretty good voice for a midget! You need to buy a bus, and hit the concert road!"

"Sure, you can be my press agent! However, I think I'll just stick to antiques, I get carsick!"

By the time Wade had come over, she had cleared the desk, washed out the refrigerator, and put some water in the trays. The papers from the filing cabinet were all stacked in wicker baskets ready for Wade to sort. Groaning, he sat down and glanced through them. "I've changed my mind; I think I'll just store these in our little barn. There probably isn't any thing I need to keep, but they'll have to be gone over, just not today." By the time he had removed the baskets, Rachael was ready to scrub and mop and soon had everything done. She brought some soft drinks from the cabin, and sat on the bench in the sunshine on the front side of the barn waiting for the movers.

Wade joined her on the bench and for a while they sat quietly, just enjoying the morning. "Wade? May I ask you a personal question? If you don't want to answer, it's okay." At his nod, she continued, "I know that your parents are truly Christians and that you attended church while you lived with them. May I ask why don't you attend now?"

Looking her in the eye, he hesitated, and then he spoke hesitantly, "My parents lived their lives with God uppermost in their thoughts. My mom still does. I admire that, just as I admire your relationship with Him. I guess the truth is, I don't know God. Everyone talks about faith; I just don't seem to have any. None of it is real to me and I won't be a hypocrite about it. It isn't something I really desire or feel I need to have a happy life." Looking at her again, he saw unshed tears in her eyes, and was touched. "Sorry, but you deserve the truth from me."

"Thank you for being so honest. Now I know how to pray for you."

They continued to sit in the sunshine quietly again, watching the birds and the clouds, just enjoying their new friendship.

When Wade looked over, Rachael was resting against the wall of the barn with her eyes closed. "So, you're starting now?"

"Nope, I was just relaxing in the sunshine and enjoying being here with you." As soon as she realized what she had said, her eyes flew open and she opened her mouth to speak again.

Placing his hand on her arm, he gently nodded. "It's okay, I like being here with you also." Settling back, he announced, "I could get used to this. It's been a busy week."

Rachael was thankful that Wade didn't take what she said too seriously. She needed to be a little more guarded around him. She had never dated much, and was finding out that it was nice to have a male friend to talk and tease with. She knew they needed to just stay as friends; however, she was very aware of him sitting next to her. She noticed how strong his hands were, and how his hair had an appealingly mussed up look. She wondered how it would be to feel his arms around her. Realizing where her thoughts were going, she told herself to STOP! There's not going to be a permanent relationship, only friendship! Not only not permanent, but no handholding, hugging, or kissing!

Soon the big moving van came along and it was the last rest they had for hours. Rachael gave instructions and directions while they unloaded the furniture from her grandmother's house. Mrs. Montgomery had been buying and selling antiques for over thirty years. Her home had been filled with special pieces that she cherished and wanted to use. She also had family pieces that had come down from her grandparents, consequentially Rachael had spent many hours pondering and planning on what she wanted to keep and what she could part with to sell in her new antique business. Some things she knew previously that she wanted in her own home, and was able to pack and mark them for her personal use. The boxes and furniture with red tape were put into Wade's truck to be taken to the cabin. The stalls were filling up, and the far side of the barn was looking like a warehouse. With only a short lunch break the movers were able to unload everything by four o'clock. Shortly after that, they were on their way with a nice tip, and some of the sandwiches and soft drinks Rose had provided for them.

Just as they had stopped for lunch earlier, an old pickup and a utility van had parked by the side road and the drivers walked over to the barn. Seeing Wade in the doorway, the burly one asked if Shelly Montgomery was around.

"Yes, but I think she wants to be called by her name, Rachael." It just took a few minutes for them to hand Rachael an envelope, telling her the boss had everything in there she needed and where did they want the van? Directing them to park it by the back door of the barn, she retrieved the keys and then took fifteen minutes to go to the bank and deposit a check. Before they drove off in the old truck, Wade had walked around to the rear of their pickup while they were out of sight and noted the license plate. He had not been impressed by either of the men, especially the one called Buddy. He thought that running the plate wouldn't be outside of his authority.

Entering her little home, Rachael was overwhelmed by the stack of things in the middle of her living room. Wade had made three trips with boxes and furniture and had just placed everything together until she could decide where it went. The high school boys had come by and Randy Stone was installing her computer station in the barn office. Bobby was helping Wade put beds together and move furniture at the cabin. By six o'clock, some of the furniture was in place and most of the boxes moved to the extra bedroom. Wade finally called a halt to the work, telling the boys they could leave and informing Rachael in a very commanding voice and a huge grin that she was also finished for the day!

"Oh, thank you Boss! I'm beat! Where did all this stuff come from? I just had a little room at Nana's."

"Well, I can personally testify to the fact that you have boxes and boxes of books and dishes. Do you know how heavy they are? I don't suppose you lifted any of them!"

Rachael gave him a smile and answered his teasing sweetly, "Hmm I don't think so, I was leaving that up to the big strong he-men!"

Reaching out his hand to help her up, they locked up and drove back to Rose's house.

Supper was rather quiet; Rose was lying down, tired from the day. She was slowing down; they discussed the fact that she didn't do as much and didn't seem interested in getting out any more. Her friends were coming to visit; almost every day someone stopped by and shared a cup of tea. Some of the ladies brought food, or a book, others serenely sat and read the Bible to her and prayed together. Rose had laughed one day when Fern came in saying she had brought food for the body and food for the soul. When they needed to cook, they had been eating a lot of soup lately. It was easy to put meat in the crock-pot and add some vegetables later on. It didn't take long to fix a salad, toast some bread, and have a good meal for whoever was hungry. Wade ate anything that was put in front of him; he was easy to please. He mentioned one day that if he developed a longing for something special he could always get it at the cafe. After dinner the phone rang and Wade had to go in to the office for a few hours. When he returned he announced that he didn't have to work until six o'clock tomorrow evening and wondered if Rachael thought she would be back from the auction by then? If so, he might… just might consider tagging along just to keep her from going bankrupt!

♦ CHAPTER SEVEN ♦

Saturday dawned clear and sunny; a beautiful March day. The early flowers were six to eight inches tall and Rachael saw them everywhere as they drove through town. When she commented, Wade groaned, "I've been meaning to tell you, or warn you I guess, depending on how you feel about it, but the Blooming Idiots voted to plant flowers at the library and… Ahem… your house."

"Seriously? How wonderful! Do I get to choose what I like? I love flowers but I'm not much of a gardener. I require plants that don't need any help from me. What a blessing!"

By the time they arrived at the huge estate where the auction was being held, they were both enjoying the drive together and looking forward to the day. Since the insurance only covered Rachael driving Mr. Andersons van, Wade had spent the time making funny little remarks about her driving, and doing a lot of 'back seat driving'. When they turned into the property, they noticed there were numerous trucks and vans already arrived and they were fortunate to find a good parking place. Wade was interested in the people and the big tents out on the lawn. By the time Rachael had signed up for two number cards they decided to have a cup of coffee and a soft drink and walk around. Some of the items on one side of the tent had a price on them designated 'FIRM' that could be bought immediately. On the other end, there were the items for the auction that would start in two hours. Wade noticed at least two security officers in uniform and what he thought were more in causal clothes.

Rachael headed towards the immediate sale side and casually walked around, making some notes and just checking everything out. When she had finished looking, she approached the sale desk and asked to talk to the person in charge. When he appeared, Rachael shook his hand and told him she had picked out eight large pieces that she liked and would take all eight if he would give her a fifteen percent discount, otherwise she wanted only two. She also had a list of items that she would buy with the same discount. When she started to walk away after being told 'sorry', he came after them in a hurry saying he had changed his mind and would sell them at discount. Handing him the paper with the numbers on it and the prices, she asked that the pieces be marked sold.

Wade was just floored! He had seen Rachael at home, serious about her life, laughing about his silly jokes, courteous to everyone, considerate of his mother and now he was seeing another side to her. She was all business! She looked like a young girl with her hair loose, wearing denim slacks and a shirt and jacket, but she was covering up a sharp mind and a decisive attitude. Leaving the immediate area, he leaned down and whispered in her ear, "Remind me not to get on the bad side of you."

Whispering back, she smiled, "I don't have a bad side!"

Wade didn't say anything, but he agreed with her. She was so different from many of the women he had met over the years, especially in college. She always had a smile, and saw the positive aspect of life. She woke up happy and stayed that way all day. Even when little irritating circumstances came along, she remained upbeat. Wade was beginning to see that she was a very special woman, and he also realized somewhat vaguely that it might have something to do with her belief in God. He could see the same thing in her that his mother exhibited. When Rose was diagnosed with cancer, she just smiled and said, 'Then there are things I want to do before I see my Savior'. Deep down he knew that he would not be able to accept a terminal illness like she had. Wade realized that he was wondering more and more about the source of peace they both seemed to have.

The area cordoned off for the auction was huge with a podium on a large platform, surrounded by bleachers. The items for auction were on display in the back and sides of the tent, and Rachael strolled along looking at the brochure, sometimes making marks on it as she walked on. They had time for a quick hot dog and drink before settling down on the right side of the bleachers. Wade reached over taking the sale pamphlet from her and studied it. Finally, he gave up and asked her to explain her notes.

"Ah, well, my dear novice. I have marked items I'm interested in, by a one two or three depending on how badly I want it, either for Mr. Anderson or myself. The one with the star I really want, you will notice it has a PTL after it. It is something I have asked the Lord for, and maybe this is the answer! The numbers represent the top price I'm willing to pay. One of the secrets of a good antique business is to determine a top price your willing to pay and stick to it. Other wise you can't gross enough to pay for the time, moving and storage. You just can't make money on impulse buying. " Shaking his head again at her organization, Wade just sat back ready to enjoy the afternoon.

The auctioneer was entertaining as well as efficient. He joked while they were moving the furniture and sale items onto the platform, keeping the momentum moving and fast. He knew about the items and gave a brief history or interesting fact about some of the large pieces. Rachael and Wade were both enjoying themselves, even with Wade groaning every time Rachael bid on something.

During a break in the proceedings, Rachael nodded towards a man across the way wearing a pair of overalls and straw hat. "Do you know him?" As Wade shook his head, she continued. "Is he going to leave you his inheritance?"

"Why, no, why would he? I'm not related to him."

"Look over there at the pretty dark haired lady in the red shirt. Do you love her?"

"Rachael! No, of course not, I don't even know her."

"Exactly! You have no relationship with him because you're not acquainted. And you don't love her because you don't know her. You didn't know me a month ago, but now we have a relationship, a friendship. That's because we have spent time together getting to know each other." Rachael smiled at Wade, and waited for him to speak.

"And your point is…?"

"The reason you don't know God and don't love Him is because you have never met him."

Wade just looked at her gentle face and then turned to the auctioneer who was speaking again. He was relieved that the auctioneer started his spiel again; he didn't know what to say to Rachael. He understood what she meant, and basically he agreed, but he still didn't see why he needed any kind of a relationship with a God that he wasn't sure existed.

Rachael was also glad the auction resumed, she wanted Wade to think about what she said and not get overwhelmed by too much information at one time. He was so intelligent; she knew that he would think about it later. *I hope I haven't overstepped here, but Father, until he wants to know you, he'll never seek you. Please help draw him to you.*

By two o'clock, Rachael had purchased two more items for her boss and one for herself. The auctioneer took a break and Rachael asked Wade if he would go back to the other side and see about loading up the van and getting the paper work done. She had totaled up the cost of accounts, hers and Mr. Andersons, and gave him the final cost. There was one more item she personally wanted, and it was supposed to be next after the break.

Just as he started to leave, he noticed a man glancing around, but his focus was on the people not the sale items. Wondering what he was looking for, Wade relaxed again and whispered to Rachael, "Just a minute, I want to watch someone." Within a few minutes the man causally climbed up the bleachers and then sat directly in back of an elderly woman sitting alone just a few seats down and over from them. As the auctioneer started to sell another piece, the man leaned down and picked up her billfold from her open purse sitting on the seat next to her, putting it in his left pocket. Wade stood up just as he did and they both proceeded to the bottom where the pickpocket turned towards the restrooms. Wade discretely took hold of his arm, and said, "You're under arrest for theft. Just walk quietly, I'm a deputy sheriff." Wade could feel the mans arm tense, but he had a good grip, and turned him around toward the outside. Locating the security officer, he turned the man over, giving the information about what he had seen. When the officer found the billfold in his pocket, he placed him in handcuffs, thanking Wade.

"I'm glad you saw this, we've been having trouble at these places. A crowd is always easy pickings, but the folks get caught up in the excitement, and just don't pay attention like they should. Sadly to say, our friend here doesn't look repentant, just disgusted that he was caught. I'd appreciated a written report, ASAP, and thank you very much!!!

Wade made his way back to the bleachers, where the lady was still watching the auction, unaware of her missing billfold. When Wade showed her his badge, and explained what had happened, she grabbed her purse, rummaging around and finally realizing Wade was telling her the truth, she left without even thanking him, heading towards the security desk in the front of the tent. Wade waved at Rachael and then left again to get her purchases grouped for loading.

He had enjoyed the day, there was a certain excitement even for those who were not buying, and the ones whose final bid was accepted for something they wanted, was sometimes hilarious. One little girl just jumped up and down when her parents bought her a large doll, only to cry when they tried to explain she had to wait until the auction was over before getting it. She had been so disappointed, that the father took her back and paid for just her doll so she could have it immediately. One day he hoped to have a sweet little girl like that to spoil.

By the time they had paid and loaded all her purchases, Rachael was worried about getting Wade back in time for work. She apologized several times, and finally Wade called Mitch to tell him he was on the road and would be a little late.

Assuring Rachael that it was not a problem, he turned the conversation to some of her purchases. "Can you tell me why you bought that basket of junk for ten dollars?"

"Sure, it was full of kitchen gadgets and a lid to a sugar bowl set that was not chipped or cracked. I have the sugar and creamer that I picked up for two dollars at a yard sale, now I have the lid and can sell the set for at least forty. That makes a twenty-eight dollar profit. It also had a saltshaker that I have a mate to that will sell for five to eight dollars. I bought a box of paperweights for twenty dollars that has an antique Eiffel tower worth forty to a collector. That is a twenty-dollar profit plus whatever else is in there of value. The big furniture was reasonably priced. There was only one other dealer interested in most of it." Then she grinned, "But he bought an armoire that was a copy and he lost about two hundred dollars in profit. He's really going to be unhappy when he gets it home."

"How did you know it was a copy and he didn't?"

"It's hard to explain; I just do! Oh, there are signs of course, the type fasteners, the glue, the stain, sanding marks, and the style. You know when you meet someone on your job and you just know they are lying to you? It's like that with me. Call it instinct or intuition or protection, whatever it is, I seem to have it. Nana used to say that I could tell a fake a block away."

"What do you mean by protection? I understand the other two, but explain that please?"

"It's Gods protection! I prayed about going and I prayed about spending Gods money today. I asked Him to keep me from impulsive buying and to stretch my money. I asked Him to allow me to make good reasonable choices for my boss and to have people willing to give me a discount. I asked Him to protect us on the road and get us home safely in time for you to go to work. And I thanked Him for your company! And… we're home; you have just twenty minutes to change while I fix you a sandwich to eat on the way to the office!"

As Wade walked through the kitchen, he grabbed the lunch bag Rachael was holding out to him, kissed her on the cheek and said, "See you tomorrow."

Then he stopped short and with his face turning red, stammered, "Rachael! I'm so sorry, I just wasn't thinking! I always kiss Mom when I leave and I did it out of habit. I'm so sorry."

With her hand on her cheek, Rachael whispered, "See you tomorrow."

Watching him go out to the squad car, she slid onto the breakfast chair and cried so hard she didn't hear Rose come into the room. As soft arms came around her and a soft kiss on her head, she looked up and said, "Oh Rose, I'm in real trouble!"

By the time Rose had brewed some tea and set some homemade banana bread on the table, Rachael had stopped crying and had gone to wash her face and hands. When she returned to the table, Rose poured their tea, and gently asked, "Has Wade hurt you Dear?"

"Oh no, but Rose, you know that I can't be interested in Wade. The Bible is very clear about a relationship between a Christian and a non-believer. We've been thrown together so much that my feelings have grown and I didn't realize how far until just now. What am I going to do?"

Pulling her into her arms, Rose hugged Rachael and then shared with her what she believed God had in store for her and Wade. "My dear, in just these few weeks, God has given me a love for you as strong as that for my son. I have peace that He has sent you to minister to Wade and that you will be his bride! When the Doctor told me that I had cancer and would not be here in two years, I asked God for three things. I have prayed for Wade all his life to realize how much he needs God and I asked my Savior to reveal Himself to Wade. And then, I wanted to see his bride and be present at his wedding! The day that you looked at the cabin and barn, I was in the shadows and saw you come through the path and pray at the picnic table. God impressed on my heart and gave me peace that He was answering my prayers." Wiping away a tear from Rachael's face, she continued, "God will never go against his word, and so I am trusting that Wade will soon open his heart to Jesus and to you. There have been and still are, many prayers on your behalf. The Garden Club ladies have a covenant to pray daily for you and for Wade."

"Thank you Rose, you're so wise, I need to let God work in Wade's life and I need for Him to show me the way to be a good testimony to Wade. I don't want to hurt him, but I will not settle for anyone, no matter how strong my feeling, if he doesn't share my love for my Savior. That is the most important thing for a marriage, and I will not jeopardize my spiritual life for a romantic one. I know that God is watching over me and will work this out to glorify Himself.

♦♦♦♦♦♦♦

After such an emotionally and physically stressful day, Rachael was tired, but she wanted to be doing something other than just sitting stewing over the situation with Wade. She knew she needed to think about it later when she was in a better frame of mind. Telling Rose she was going to the barn to set up her accounts from the sale today, she drove the van over to the back of the barn and parked it with the back next to the rear barn wall. Since she couldn't get it unloaded until the boys came to help after school Monday, she thought this would be the safest way to park. The rear doors couldn't be opened and she carefully locked the front doors. She slipped through the path to get a soft drink from the cabin, then retuned to the barn.

The barn was really eerie in the dark; Rachael wished she had brought a flashlight to help her find the light switch. She groped around for minutes trying to find the switch and finally touched the panel. She would have to practice learning which switch controls each light, she thought as the front lights came on. Finally she kept trying until she found the rear ones. They gave her enough light to proceed to the office where she knew the switch was just inside the door. Sitting down in the chair, she let the tears fall again. *Oh God I don't know what to think. Is Rose hearing your voice and I'm not? Why would you tell her something and not me? Is my coming here part of your plan for my life? Is Wade? I need your peace Father, please help me to know how to share your love with Wade.*

Turning on her computer, Rachael began to set up the accounts that she would need to keep track of her purchases for Mr. Anderson. Just as she finished listing the purchases for today, her cell phone rang, startling her. After checking the caller I.D., she cleared her throat and tried to sound cheerful. It was Wade asking her if she would mind if he went over to her cabin to pick up a notebook he had left on her counter; he needed a phone number from it. He still had a key, but wouldn't go with out her permission.

Wade unlocked the cabin door and turned on the light, knowing that usually he could have walked around without them, but now there were boxes and furniture all over the floor. As he reached over to get the notebook, he happened to glance down at the wastebasket. Puzzled, he reached down and picked it up, looking at the object lying on the bottom. Picking up what looked like a cigarette butt, he sniffed it, immediately realizing that someone had been using drugs here. He felt his chest burn like someone was squeezing the life out of him. He knew that no one else besides Rachael could have been here since last night. When they had left, he had collected all the trash, wrappings, and boxes and put them outside to be picked up. He remembered emptying this basket and putting it back down by the cabinets. Could Rachael be doing drugs?

Everything in him shouted 'NO', but the evidence was here in his hand. He carefully took a paper towel, wrapped the short smoke and placed it in his pocket. Feeling absolutely limp from disappointment, he decided to check and see if she had been here. Calling her on her cell again, he asked her, "Did you happen to see my notebook? Were you here earlier?"

"Just for a minute, I picked up a soda, and walked around a little deciding where things were going to go. Why? Can't you find your notebook?"

"Ah... Here it is, sorry to bother you- see you later."

Going back out to his car, he felt physically ill. There had to be some other explanation. His thoughts were jumbled and painful. I just don't think she could fool me like this. She's so sweet and... man! I haven't met anyone that I've ever gotten along with as easily as I have her. If she knew how badly I wanted to hold her hand like a couple of kids while we sat on the bench the other day, she would probably faint. There isn't any sense in trying to deny the attraction I feel toward her. I like being near her and wish we could spend even more time together. I wonder if this is the beginning of love? After all these years when I haven't been interested in even meeting anyone special, she comes along. Oh well, no matter how I feel, I need to stay away until I know for certain where she stands on drugs. What a mess! I'd better read her records again. With her brother in prison for drugs, this looks bad. We have so many drugs in this county that we don't need any more. I just can't believe this!

By the time Wade had a chance to sit down at the computer in the office, it was after one A.M. He pulled up Russell Montgomery on the police access and began to read again. By following links, he finally got to the arrest record. The witness reports all agreed and had compiled a report that they all signed.

The shooter entered the antique store which Mrs. Montgomery owned. She and her granddaughter, Shelly Montgomery were working and there were three customers browsing around. He was wearing a red sweatshirt with a hood, and light jeans, white running shoes. Witness number three recognized him as the grandson of Mrs. Montgomery. When the man entered, he started waving a gun around, shouting and not making any sense. Witnesses one and two ducked behind furniture and tried to get closer to the front as he walked to the back. The third had been standing close to the door, but rather hidden behind a large chifferobe. When the man passed him shouting at his grandmother, he was able to escape out the door and call 911. The other two witnesses said that he shouted 'I want your money old lady! I'm tired of Shelly getting handouts and sponging off you when I should be getting all the money.' Mrs. Montgomery said, 'Russell, put the gun down, I won't give you any money to buy drugs with.' He waved the gun at Miss Shelly and said 'Give me what ever you have hidden here; I know you're selling drugs and I want whatever you have.' Then Miss Shelly said, 'I'm a Christian, You know I don't use drugs. I would never destroy my body that way.'

Wade could just see her saying that in the face of danger, he just couldn't believe she was involved. He continued reading the report.

The two remaining witnesses reported that the man was waving the gun around at the two women and cursing them.

He acted 'spaced out'. His eyes were 'funny' and his speech 'slurred'. Mrs. Montgomery waved Miss Shelly back and started to walk closer to him. He told her to stay back and 'give him what he wanted, or he would shoot them and then he could get it all.' Mrs. Montgomery said 'No, Russell, you won't inherit from me, not a dime.' When she said that, he just went 'crazy' and pushed things over and ranted and cursed. It was really loud; he was shooting, two shots aimed high, and breaking things and shoving things over. Then Mrs. Montgomery took another step closer and he shot her in the leg. The gunshots were really loud! She fell down; blood was already staining her clothes when Miss Shelly went toward her. He grabbed her arm and pulled her up. She cried out in pain when he grabbed her. Then he said. 'Where's the stuff? I know you have some here. Give it to me or I'll do the same thing to you.' He hit her once with his other hand, and she fell against a table, crying out, and you could hear a bone break. Then the police entered the front and back doors, two in front and two in back, pointed guns at him, and said, 'Police! Drop your weapon or we'll shoot!' The man jerked Miss Shelly's arm and pulled her up in front of him again, but there was too much furniture in the store for him to go anywhere. As he turned to look around, one of the policeman which had gotten to the side, shot him in the arm that was holding the gun, knocking it onto the floor. He screamed and shoved Miss Shelly down. The cops got him down and put handcuffs on him. The paramedics came in to help Mrs. Montgomery. The blood was pouring out of her leg; she was trying to put pressure on it. Miss Shelly had been pushed down and had hit her head. She was on the floor unconscious. They were both taken out to the ambulance. The police had us write down what had happened. We all agree on this.

Whew! That was something! Wade could read between the lines and see in his mind just how it went down. He had been on many calls like that and it was scary! The civilians were usually so scared that they were more detrimental than helpful. The police officer that shot Russell's arm really took a chance. He must be an excellent shot.

He sorted through other files until he came to the court records. Russell had been arrested for drug possession and dealing before this happened. But no matter how he tried to white wash it, even if it was by a spaced out druggie, Rachael had been accused of selling drugs. Shutting down the reports, he leaned back in the chair. Now what do I do?

Suddenly remembering getting the license plate of the drivers, he pulled up the van and truck registrations. The Van was licensed to George Anderson and the truck to West 'Buddy' Riller. This was getting in deeper and deeper. Anderson was under surveillance for drug dealing. The one called Buddy had an arrest record for petty things, and one term in prison for drugs. What was Rachael doing associating with these thugs? They were scum! Was he wrong about her? Wade just couldn't fathom how she could be involved in anything illegal. He realized that his emotions were going to jeopardize his impartiality if he wasn't careful and he knew he needed to back away and go slowly. She wasn't at fault for her brother's crimes, but doing business with known drug dealers and felons? This was more than he could account for.

♦ CHAPTER EIGHT ♦

Sunday Rachael found a note from Wade by the coffee pot saying he had gotten in at four- thirty and would be sleeping in. Mentioning it to Rose at breakfast, Rachael suggested they go to the hotel dinning room after church and use the discount coupon Fern had given her. She knew that both the ladies had hoped that she would ask Wade but that was just not going to happen! She had decided that even though she was drawn to him, she would not make any excuses to be with Wade or do anything that remotely looked like a date. She thought this would be a good time to use the coupon and give Rose a chance to visit with other friends that would be dining there. There might not be many more chances for her to go to 'The Hotel'; Rose was failing; she could see it. The first time Rachael had met her, Rose had been animated and planning on how Rachael's home would be, discussing what she thought would be nice. Now she asked about everything, but her interest was not as strong.

At the end of the services, the Pastor mentioned that the bookstore was open today. This was the first time Rachael had heard about being able to buy discounted books, so she was pleased and interested in seeing what they had since she loved to read and study. The small room was filled with discounted Bibles and Christian books. Rachael would have loved to spend more time looking but Rose was looking weary, so she purchased a small new testament for Wade and went to get the car.

The hotel was crowded, but Rachael had called to tell Fern she was bringing Rose and they had a table waiting. Rose was tired, but she still beamed at the attention she got from the staff and diners alike. It was obvious that she was well liked in town and an important part of the history of the community. Rachael enjoyed a wonderful salad and soup bar and Rose ordered just a small soup and a muffin. By the time they returned home, Rachael had to help Rose into her room, where she could change into a robe and lie down.

The rest of the day Rachael rested and then started packing up her things in the bedroom. She had decided that even though the cabin was not completely ready, that she would start staying there at night. The beds had been put together and she had seen the box containing linens. She would be fine there and it would give her the time to sort and unpack as she felt inclined. She carried out her suitcases, packed her car, and drove over to the cabin.

Entering her new home, she realized that she was going to miss being with Rose and Wade. It felt empty in the little cabin. There were boxes stacked all around, and the clutter was overwhelming! When she had packed, she had no idea of exactly what she could use in her new home, so she packed things from her grandmothers that she wanted to keep. Now that she was in the small cabin, there would not be room for everything. Hopefully by the time the boys came after school tomorrow she would have a better idea what to keep here. She made up the bed and found a box of towels. As she unpacked her suitcases, she prayed for God to use her in this little town, and to be a part of Wade's understanding the Gospel.

By the time she returned to get dinner for Rose, Wade's car was gone so she assumed that he had gone to work. They were still short handed and the men were filling in extra hours. Hopefully he would get back on schedule soon.

Rose was sitting in the sunroom reading when Rachael looked for her. She spent some time talking about the church service and then shared that she had bought the Bible for Wade. "I found a bookmarker that reads 'Faith cometh by hearing and hearing by the word of God.' I placed it in the front of the book of John. Maybe he will read some of it."

Rose was so touched that she held out her hand for Rachael and they prayed right then that the Spirit of God would touch Wade and give him a hunger for truth.

Rachael spent the evening with Rose, listening to her reminisce about her husband and Wade as a little boy. She told about his childhood and the family activities they had enjoyed together. Helping Rose to her room, Rachael offered to help her get settled but Rose wanted to be as independent as possible.

Walking from room to room in the cabin, Rachael was just filled with thankfulness to God for providing a new place for her to live. She moved a few things and unpacked a couple of boxes, then she gathered her Bible, tablet, and pen and started on the Sunday School lesson for next week. Today had been an introduction to the book of Revelation. Mr. Easton had told about the Apostle John's relationship with the Lord, and how privileged he was that Jesus chose him to reveal the end times to Christians. He gave the time line and what was happening in the world at the time it was written. Now Rachael wanted to study the first chapter and be prepared next week. Hopefully she would come across the box with her study books and would be able to use them also. After spending a couple of hours reading and looking up scriptures, Rachael called it a night and after checking the locks went to bed, leaving the hall light on. There were just too many obstacles in the way if she needed to get up in the night!

Monday was a busy day! She ran errands in town, stocked up her cabinets, refrigerator, and laundry shelves. She also stopped by the local animal shelter and found just the puppy she wanted! When she walked through the kennels, a little beige longhaired puppy jumped up and down; she was so excited at getting attention! The worker let her out and she just climbed all over Rachael, giving kisses and walking on her lap. She had already stolen Rachael's heart! It didn't take long to get the paper work done and take home her little companion. She played with her and then started on the boxes in the bedrooms. By noon she had gotten her room straightened and her clothes put away. Most of them had to go in the laundry to be freshened up and the wrinkles pressed out. Taking her lunch to the front porch, she was enjoying the nice weather when Wade drove up. Opening the gate, he walked up to the porch, but before he could put his foot on the first step, the little ball of fur tackled him, yapping excitedly. Reaching down he grabbed it and held it up with one hand. "What in the world is this?" By then the little puppy was up against his chest licking his face and biting his mustache.

Rachael just crossed her arms, trying to look very innocent and serious. "Why Deputy, what does it look like?"

"It looks like a little ragmop! What are you doing with this thing?" He asked trying to look stern.

"This is my new puppy! You suggested to me that I should get a dog, and after the silence and lonely house last night, I thought it was a good idea."

"Rachael, I suggested you get a dog! Not a toy! I was thinking of a collie or shepherd not some little yappy fur ball!"

By then, he was getting licked and climbed over… and he was trying hard not to smile.

"Well, you must admit, she's a good guard dog; she let me know you were here."

"Not until I was on top of it and… wow… I was really scared… just shaking in my boots! I can't believe you got that thing. Where did you get it?"

"In town, at the shelter; I'm going to volunteer there when I'm not working. They always need help."

Wade set the puppy down and watched as she jumped up the steps and onto Rachael's lap.

Giving her a disgusted look, he inquired. "I don't suppose its name is Tiger or Rover."

"Sorry, no." Rachael lowered her head to give the puppy a hug so Wade wouldn't see her grin. "Her name is Posey."

"What!!!" With that, Wade just turned around and walked away shaking his head. Rachael thought she heard something about another blooming idiot!

By the time he had gone out the gate, Rachael was laughing so hard tears were coming down her face. Giving Posey a hug, she told her. "I know that you aren't what he had in mind, but you're my puppy and just what I want! I'm going to spoil you and pamper you and we're going to be the best friends ever. We're not going to need anyone else to make us happy Posey; it's just you and me from now on!"

Humming a hymn, Rachael accomplished so much in the afternoon that she was ready for the highschoolers when they came. Bobby had an old car that made a lot of noise, and Posey had no trouble in announcing that they had arrived. When they came through the gate, Posey ran to meet them and Bobby scooped her up and nuzzled her. Randy just walked on and she heard him tell Bobby to keep that mutt out of his way or she wouldn't be around long. Bobby handed her over to Rachael and politely asked what she wanted done. But Randy shuffled his feet and glanced everywhere but at her. She motioned them into the house, but as Randy passed she glimpsed his face and his eyes were glazed.

Rachael reached out and stopped Randy at the door. Taking his face in her hands, she gazed into his eyes. "Randy, I want you to leave; Bobby, take him home! I'll not have anyone in my house that uses drugs! If I ever see you in this condition again I'll report you to Deputy Marsdon. You're too precious to God to ruin your life this way."

"Hey lady, I's fine. Jus' a 'ittle pick me up! Whataya want dome? How 'bout this lamp." He started to snatch it, but Bobby grabbed him and pulled him out the door.

He glanced back at Rachael. "I'm sorry Miss Rachael, I tried to get him to wait, but he won't listen."

"I think you'd better start choosing your friends more selectively. He'll never listen to you; all he'll do is get you into trouble. Will you come back later if you can?"

Now what? Should she tell Wade? He already knew that Randy did drugs. Rachael remembered that when she asked Wade about paying the boys for helping, he said, 'No thanks, it was taken care of' and when she asked him if they were doing community service, he had nodded. Obviously, the punishment wasn't doing much good. What he needed was to get his life turned around. *I wonder if going to church counts as community service. I might ask Wade next time I see him.* Setting Posey down, she returned to her work.

Now that she was in her house she wanted to start going to the Bible Study on Wednesday nights, but the movers would be bringing the furniture and boxes from her grandmothers antique shop in the afternoon. They would have to be stored in the barn and she would be busy getting things put where she wanted. She had hired a moving company to pack and store the merchandise from the store so she didn't know exactly what was in each box as she did with the household contents. Maybe she could start going next Wednesday.

Mr. Anderson had contacted her to let her know that Buddy and Sam would be here late Thursday to pick up the furniture she had bought. He wanted to know if they could sleep in the barn Thursday night. They would leave first thing Friday.

When Bobby returned, they managed to remove the purchases from the van that went into Rachael's house; she was thrilled with the wooden butcher-block island she had purchased for her kitchen. They removed the things for her shop, and left the big dressers, armoires, and trunks for the van drivers to deal with. Then they returned to the cabin and sat down on the front porch with a soda. Rachael had been praying all afternoon about Bobby and Randy. She felt like Bobby was more open, and would probably listen so she asked him whether he ever attended church.

Surprised, he shook his head, "Naw, my mom works all the time, and she don't care about going."

After chatting about his home life, Rachael asked him what he knew about Jesus. Again, he looked surprised, but answered. "Not much. Christmas and Easter... I don't know..." he shrugged, "It doesn't have anything to do with me."

Just what she wanted! Rachael started talking about how Jesus came for everyone, born of a virgin; the God-Man lived and died for all of us. She explained that the Bible teaches that 'all have sinned' and fall short of God's righteousness. So He loved us enough to make a way to live with Him forever. Jesus stepped in and paid the debt for the sin that keeps us out of heaven. So that when we trust in Him and accept His payment, God sees us as sinless as Jesus. It assures us of a home with him forever. Heaven is a benefit! Jesus is the way! He will love you, guide you, and live inside of you forever. You just have to trust Him as your Savior and Lord."

Bobby had plenty of questions. He still didn't understand a lot, but Rachael took her time to explain everything, using the scriptures from the Bible so he would know it wasn't just her idea; it was Gods. One of the main things she wanted him to understand was that God did not make puppets to worship him. "He gives us a choice, and if we choose to love and worship and serve Him, there are many benefits that we receive."

Before he left, he had agreed to attend church with her on Sunday, and go for Pizza after. She suggested that he get Randy to come, but he shook his head, "Randy doesn't listen to anyone, he just does what he wants. His dad's always working and isn't home. I try to keep him out of trouble, but he's doing more drugs all the time."

Rachael found that living in a new town didn't mean there weren't new requests on her prayer list. She spent time each evening praying for the new people she had met.

By the time the movers arrived on Wednesday, Rachael's cabin looked like home. There were still boxes in the guest room, but the main living room was arranged the way she wanted it. She had made a grouping in front of the fireplace on the left wall and had her roll top desk in the front right corner. She placed her grandmother's rocker in front of the window on the left so she could look out. She had used many thing from her grandmothers, some were antiques and some were newer things that she was able to mix in to give it a cozy look. She had placed an antique dish rack on the wall of the dining area and placed her great grandmother's Currier and Ives dishes on the shelves. When her phone rang, letting her know the movers were at the barn, she locked up and put Posey on a leash before walking over to direct the men.

They were very efficient and placed the bedroom furniture in the stalls and the boxes in the middle. The large pieces were put in the double stall by the door, and before long, they were on their way. Bobby came by and helped her move some things where she wanted them and she was able to share about the gospel a little more. He asked some of the questions everyone wanted to know, about hypocrites, people who say they are Christians but don't act any differently than others.

"Everyone makes a choice Bobby, about how they will live, what they will do. Even though some people choose to follow the Lord, they don't keep the relationship strong and they fall back into old ways. The way to stay strong is to read your Bible and let Jesus lead you every day. I have never ever regretted choosing Christ. He gives me such joy and peace; things that you may not be able to see on the outside, but inside I know I'm loved and protected by Him."

Joining Rose for dinner, Rachael shared her teasing Wade about Posey. Rose was charmed with Posey, and enjoyed having her on her lap. Posey seemed to understand that she needed to be gentle with the older lady. Wade had mentioned Posey to his mother and she enjoyed hearing about his response to the little puppy. "Wade actually loves animals and he finally admitted that she was really cute and he could see why you picked her out. She'll be a good companion for you."

Now that she wasn't staying there, she didn't have the opportunity to see Wade as often, which was one of the reasons she had moved so soon. She would have liked to stay longer to help with Rose, but they had a lady coming in next week to stay full time. Wade wanted to spend more time with his mother, but right now, their shifts were extended and he was either gone or sleeping. Rachael left the New Testament on the pillow of Wade's bed, hoping that he would not be angry, but that God could soften his heart enough for him to read the scriptures.

Her mind had been so confused lately. She recognized that she had feelings for Wade. She really enjoyed the time they spent together; he was sensitive and interesting. They seemed to be able to relate to each other, with out compromising their own ideas. He could relax and enjoy the auctions even though he was not particularly interested in them. Now that she had moved into her own place, maybe things would settle down. She could get back into a better routine of reading and studying her Bible and could attend the study on Wednesday nights. It would help her to sort out her relationship with Wade if she was listening to the Lord.

She also realized that she owed him an apology. Even though she had been teasing, she shouldn't have said she would never be afraid of him. He certainly was a professional in his job! The relationship with his mother came from love, not weakness. She could see the respect from the other officers, including the Sheriff. He also showed integrity in his public and personal life. She would never have known about his part in the arrest of the pickpocket if she hadn't read it in the paper. Even though she had asked him about the lady, he had just shrugged and commented that she was wanted outside. The newspaper had given him the credit for apprehending the thief and turning him over to the security officer. They credited him with catching one of the main leaders who were working the fairs and sales in the area. She had noticed him observing his surrounding whether he was at the café or sales with her. His work was not just a job to him, it was a way he could help others. She knew that he would be the first one to call if she ever needed help!

Thursday, Rachael took Posey in the car with her to town. They stopped at the library and the hardware store before going on to the café for lunch. Rachael was careful to roll the windows down to prevent Posey from getting too warm and waved good by to her. Mary from Wade's office was meeting her for lunch, something they had planned after church on Sunday.

As soon as she entered and found a seat, Donna brought her a pot of tea and a cup. "Guess you're all moved in and have stuff stored at the barn. You must have a lot of furniture to need that big barn. Do you want to order or wait for Wade?"

Trying to keep from grinning Rachael set her straight. "Actually Donna, I'm meeting Mary for lunch. I'll wait until she comes in if that's okay."

"Sure. Whatever!"

When Mary came in, Donna brought water and took their orders, but before she left, Rachael asked her if she worked every Sunday morning, or was she able to go to church.

"Church?" A wistful look came on her face, "I work every day; six to four in the afternoon or noon to midnight and go home and crash. I don't have time to go anywhere."

"Oh my! How can you work those long hours? You must be exhausted by the time you go home. Do you have family to take care of?"

Shifting from one foot to the other, Donna nodded. "I have a son, he's a teenager now. I worry about him after school when I can't be there, but there's no choice. I'm doing the best I can by myself."

After she had walked away, Mary told Rachael that she had been praying for Donna and her son for years. "He's a sweet kid, but he's getting in with the wrong crowd. He got in some trouble a few years ago, and it seemed to wake him up, but he has a friend that's doing drugs and it won't be long until he really gets in trouble."

Putting two and two together, Rachael asker her if it happened to be Bobby, and at Mary's nod, she shared that he was helping her and that she had been able to explain the gospel. "He's promised to come to church Sunday. Can you tell me where the teen class is located and who the teacher is? I was thinking about giving him a heads up that Bobby would be there. Of course, he may not show but it never hurts to have someone looking out for him."

Rachael was curious about the teens in town. "Is there a drug problem here? This is such a little town, I wouldn't think it would be a problem."

"Please don't quote me, but actually there is a substantial problem with the teenagers and drugs. The night Wade was gone until three in the morning? They busted up a campfire in the woods north of here that had a bunch of kids there. By the time they got the call and responded, the kids were gone, but there was evidence of booze and drugs there. They took fingerprints so they know who was there, but they can't do anything until they see them. There are some other problems involved with it that make it rather sensitive also. But Wade is really doing everything he can to stop the selling here."

"The 'sensitive problem' was helping me at the cabin and I had to ask him to leave. Should I tell Wade?"

"Oh Rachael I'm so sorry! I know you don't want to get put in the middle. How about I just mention it and see what he does with the info?"

When she returned to the car, Rachael was glad to be greeted with hugs and kisses and wags; Posey was getting attached quickly and so was Rachael.

♦ CHAPTER NINE ♦

By the time the men sent from Mr. Anderson called and said they were coming into town, Rachael had contacted Wade and asked permission for them to stay all night in the barn. He didn't seem very happy about it, but gave permission. Actually she wasn't too happy about it either, but as long as they left in the morning and didn't steal her merchandise, she didn't see that it was much different than sleeping in the van. She had made sure though that her office was locked before she had left in the afternoon.

Shortly, the van pulled up in the back and parked next to her van. She had left room for the ramp to be lowered, and they did also. After unlocking the door, she showed them the pieces that were going to be sent out, and had them sign for them and give receipts. Buddy did the talking; what little there was. He was definitely taciturn and rather tired acting. After telling them to leave her keys to the van in the barn on the counter, she asked them to keep the doors locked and to lock the rear door of the barn when they left in the morning.

Wade parked his car along the road, and then called into Laurel that he would be out of contact for thirty minutes, giving her his location. Taking his flashlight and checking his gun, he approached the trees by the vans in back of the barn. Rachael had told him the men would be moving the furniture from her van in to the other one and then would be staying there to sleep and leaving early in the morning. He watched them for a few minutes, trying to figure out what they were doing. Instead of moving the furniture from one van to the other, they were taking the pieces into the barn for a few minutes, and then carrying it to the other van. As he was trying to figure out why they were doing this, they went inside and shut the door. Taking advantage of the few minutes, he looked into their van, trying to see in the dark. He was skeptical about turning on the flashlight, and he knew there wasn't much time. He jumped down just as he heard their voices and the door open again. When they re-entered the barn with another piece, he crept into the van and ran his hands over the furniture, finding underneath the trim of the bottom of a tall bookcase, what felt like a plastic bag. He hurried off just in time, and rolled under the ramp. Wiggling under the van while they were inside, he hid until they had another piece in the barn and he took a chance with his penlight and noted down the license plate number before going around to the side of the barn. The window was just too high to see much and there was furniture in the way, but he could tell that they turned over a tall dresser and were doing something to it that he couldn't see. Then they put it upright and carried it out. Hiding in the shadows on the side of the barn, he heard one of them ask, "What time are we heading out?"

"Early, I don't want'a be driving this stuff any longer than I have too. The sooner we get going the sooner we're done. We should make the state line by mid morning."

The other man remarked, "I don't know why the pilot can't do a drop there, it would save us from having to drive all over."

"You idiot! Then we wouldn't be making big bucks! Besides, you can't just fly planes low everywhere without being seen. This place is perfect."

Hearing them shut up the vans, Wade waited until they were inside and then quietly made his way to the squad car.

Rolling his car down the road before he turned the ignition on, Wade turned around and headed into town. Laurel informed him that Mitch was on his way in from the lake where he had been checking out more reports of lights and noise. After asking her to have Mitch bring coffee and meet him in town, he tried to piece together what he had seen. No matter what, he had a lot to tell Mitch. And he would have to tell him the rest of what he had learned from the criminal report. There was no way that he could do his job honestly and not tell Mitch.

Turning into the bank parking lot he made a U-turn and parked facing the street, still trying to sort through what he'd seen. Within a few minutes, Mitch pulled up along side and passed a coffee over to Wade.

"What's up?"

Wade proceeded to tell his boss what he had seen and then drank his coffee while Mitch filtered it through other information.

"Okay, Wade good job! I know this looks bad, but just wait until we get it over with and then see where Rachael fits in. I need for you to go off duty now; go home and sleep. I want you to be ready to follow them in your personal vehicle when they leave in the morning. I'll contact the sheriff in the next county and fill them in so they can get a man on it at the line. Be sure you have your cell phone for communication. I'll get the paperwork in and put a spy tracker on their van before it gets light. I enjoy getting the judge out of bed for a warrant! Maybe we can track where they go and drop off the drugs and at least that will give the guys a chance to track it from there. What we need is to backtrack it. Maybe they can put an undercover in and find out when the next shipment is on the move."

"I would assume it's when Rachael has another load for them."

"Right! Well, we need to know that, you'll have to keep tabs on her and what she's doing. Meanwhile we can do an aerial view and try to figure out where the drop is. Go on, get some sleep, and don't lay awake worrying about Rachael. It'll all work out."

Wade left a note for his mother, and laid out some clothes for the morning. After setting his alarm, he tossed and turned. Finally, he turned the light on and picked up the Bible that Rachael had placed on his pillow. Opening where the bookmarker indicated, he read the first few pages of John. Was Jesus really come from God? Was He truly the Son of God? How can that be? What makes Him different than we are? What did these fishermen see in Him that they wanted to follow him? What power did He have that we don't have? Finally, he drifted off to a restless sleep, but when the alarm went off at 5:00, he was able to be dressed and ready in a few minutes. Before he left, he made ham sandwiches and picked up the thermos of last nights coffee. His truck was full of gas, so he parked on the road where he couldn't be seen and waited.

Watching the rear of the barn, his thoughts kept returning to Rachael and the police reports. This is a mess! It's different when it's someone you … what are my feelings? Admit it, you jerk, you're falling in love finally, and she may be a felon. At least she's probably involved with trafficking. Maybe using? No wonder Mitch was willing to be easy on Randy. Except; it hasn't helped, he's still doing drugs and it has to be stopped. We don't need any more drugs brought in our county! What can I do? There's nothing I can do I guess. If she's involved, then she's not the person I think she is, and I wouldn't love that person. But I just don't believe she's involved. She's so sincere. I may not believe like she does, but it is obvious that she believes in God and that she puts Him first. She seems to have that relationship but more than that, she has an inner peace just like Mom does. How many times have I heard Mom say, 'God is in charge of my life, whatever happens, happens for a reason and I'll just trust in Him, He wants His best for me.' How could you trust in someone you've never seen; it's hard enough to trust the ones you can see? He was thankful when the drivers got into the van so he could concentrate on police business instead of personal. He let them get ahead and then drove behind them.

Wade had been following the van for almost two hours. They had exited for food once and then gotten back on the road. The state line was coming up in a few miles and Wade was watching to see if anyone was following him yet. The DEA and the local sheriff were supposed to pick him up about now. As they passed an exit ramp, Wade noticed a car parked at the top begin to move and pull in place behind him. He picked up his cell phone just as it rang.

"Marsdon here."

"Well now, Deputy, I have you in my sight, but more important, I have that nasty van in view. There's also a truck in front of them and we are on your spy tracker. I think Partner, we have it covered and if you want to just mosey back to your little part of the world, we'll take over from here!"

"Hey Tucker, noticed you on top and made a hole for you. We're hoping you can do some good today, we'll let you know if anything happens on our end."

"Ours too! Adios Amigo!"

Wade exited and crossed over to catch the highway back to the south. He called Mary to let her know he was headed back to town and asked her to call Rachael and see if she was busy this morning. If not, could Mary give her directions and have her meet him at the local flea market in a couple hours. Maybe he could find out something pertinent to the case. The case! It was now a case with a full investigation. This was the first time his personal life had interfered with his work, and he was having trouble coping with it. He just had to face the fact that his feelings were clouding his judgment about Rachael, but he just couldn't believe that she was involved. If she was, then she was the biggest hypocrite he had ever met. But the evidence of her involvement was growing.

Wade dropped down on the bench where Rachael would be meeting him, and put his head in his hands. He had a nagging headache from lack of sleep and too much stress. His mind kept going back to what he had read last night. If Jesus was the Son of God somehow, not just a man, then what did that mean to him? He remembered people saying, you need to trust Christ. Trust Him for what? Rachael had said that heaven was a bonus, so what about now? What possible benefit was there now, and how important was it? He was so engrossed in his thoughts that he hadn't realized that Rachael had sat down beside him.

"You look like you have the weight of the world on your shoulders, Wade; is there something I can do?" Rachael was thrilled to see the look on Wade's face when he turned toward her. It was a look that lit up his face. It was obvious that he was glad to see her.

"It's nothing that can't be put aside now that you're here; come on! I'm starving and they have the best chili dogs in town. This is the first day they're open for the season, and I have been waiting impatiently. You'll get to meet another of our local 'characters'! Plus! I have two hours at your service Ma'am to wander around looking at junk!"

Laughing they entered the building that had been converted from a warehouse into the Flea market. Since it was Friday, it was crowded but not like it would be the next day. Wade directed Rachael to the left where he stopped at the food court. The vender behind the counter greeted Wade by name and said. "Two chili dogs, hold the onions coming right up." Handing Wade two drinks and setting two plates of fries and hot dogs on the counter he shook his head at Wade when he handed him a twenty-dollar bill. "This here's my gift to you and the little lady. That's why you didn't get any onions this time! She sure is a looker, be sure you keep 'er close. Those kind are hard to find. Your kid's'll be right nice looking between the two of you."

Rachael picked up the drinks and headed towards the tables, her face as red as a tomato. Everyone in the area must know all about me she thought. Maybe though they could see better than she and Wade could. All I see is obstacles that no one except God can work out.

Wade waited until she offered thanks for the food and fellowship, and then took a huge bite from the end of his bun. "I don't know what he puts in the sauce, but it just makes the sandwich. I miss the onions though. Do you like it?"

Grinning she nodded, "Yes and it's a good thing, since I didn't have any say about it. Does he always give you want he wants you to have?"

"Yup! He sells other things that are good also, but he decides what he sells to each customer. Rather unique, but the food is so good no one complains."

They wondered around for a long time, Rachael browsing and buying a few things which Wade carried in the bag she had brought. She was enjoying the time spent with Wade in a relaxed atmosphere and they laughed and joked as they walked along. They tried on Mexican hats, and hunting helmets, but Rachael shook her head when Wade picked up a hula skirt with a raised eyebrow. The far end of the building was set apart for large furniture and as they approached, Rachael reached into her bag to pull out the list from Mr. Anderson. It was a list of furniture and ultimate prices beside it. They continued to walk around and found two dressers, but the vendor wanted more than she was willing to pay.

Wade asked her about her job with Mr. Anderson, how it came about. He also asked if the drivers got off okay today, and if everything had worked out with them. He casually asked if they lived close or did they have to drive a long way to pick up merchandise?

"I don't know anything about them. I've seen them pick up furniture at Nana's but that's all. My only contact is with Mr. Anderson; I have nothing to do with anything else. I just make sure the furniture is available for him to move. The drivers are rather rough and I never had any reason to speak to them before. I haven't been to the barn yet today, so I guess everything's okay. If not, I know how to get a hold of them."

By the time Wade needed to leave to get his paper work turned in at the office, Rachael had purchased two large pieces of furniture that they put in her van. She also had two carryall bags full of little things that had caught her eye. It was a fun day and one she hoped they could repeat. Following Wade home, she prayed for him, asking God to open the way to speak to him again. He had not said anything about the Bible she had left on his bed, and she didn't know what he thought about her giving it to him. He must not have been angry or upset, since he had been the one to initiate spending the morning together.

After they unloaded the van, standing by the back door Wade remarked that it was a beautiful day. The sun was shining, the trees were starting to bud out, and there was a wonderful spring breeze.

"How do you know there is a breeze?"

"Pardon me?"

She repeated her question and puzzled, Wade answered, "I can feel it."

"Can you see it? Hold it?"

"Well no… but I can feel it blowing on my face."

"Ah ha! You can't see it or hold it, but you know that there's a breeze because you can see the results."

"Well… yes, I can see the trees moving, and the clouds are being blown across the sky."

"So you know there's a breeze because you can see what it does. Well, my friend, that's just like God and His Spirit. You can't see Him or touch Him physically, but you can see the results of Him everywhere. He made the clouds and the breeze, and the trees that are being blown by the breeze. He's the Creator, and we can know that He is because we see the results of His handiwork. And spiritually we can trust Him because He is in charge of the things we see and the things we don't see. You're looking at God with your head; you need to just trust your heart." Smiling, she patted him on the arm and walked toward the path leading through the trees.

Rachael prayed as she walked home, anxious to have Wade understand and recognize that God was alive and that He is the creator. Smiling she unlocked the door to let Posey out. It was so wonderful coming into the house and having that little bundle of fur rush at her. She scooped her up and received licks, hugs and woofs, just as though she was the most important person in the world to the little dog. Telling her to sit, she attached her leash to the harness and they walked to the barn, stopping to let Posey check out everything on the way.

What a mess! There was furniture everywhere; she already had enough to start her business, thanks to Nana leaving the house furnishings and the shop to her. She was anxious to start, but realized it would take months to get everything cleaned and straightened out and ready. She gazed at the two pieces she had purchased today; one was a bookcase and the other a tall dresser. They were in good condition; they just needed a little polishing. She had decided to put things in place and then go back later and clean everything, it would just take time to get it all done. Posey had been running around 'sniffing and snooping', leaving little paw prints on the dust on the floor by the back door. Rachael went into the office to record the bookcase for Mr. Anderson when Posey came in acting funny. She was stumbling and falling, her head was shaking and she was whimpering. Her eyes looked glazed and when Rachael picked her up, she tried to bite her! Locking the office, Rachael grabbed her keys, grateful that she had left her car here earlier, and drove into town to the vet where she had gotten Posey's shots. Rushing in, she explained to the receptionist that she had been in the barn, and maybe she had gotten into something, although Rachael had not seen anything that would have hurt her. The barn had not had any chemicals in it, and it had been swept and washed just a few days ago.

Rachael waited anxiously while they ran tests on her little dog. Finally the Doctor came out and reported, "Whatever caused this, she'll be fine, I want to keep her overnight just in case; we've given her some meds and I'd like to keep an eye on her. You can come by in the morning and get her."

Dejected, Rachael drove home alone; thankful Posey would be okay, but wondering what had caused this. Maybe there was something in the barn or the pathway that she got into. She would look when she returned home later. She drove on to Rose's house to have dinner with her, telling her about their day and the problem with Posey.

As she was driving home later, she noticed Wade's car in the back of the barn, and drove in to see why he was there. When she opened the door, she found him kneeling on the floor with a knife scraping something onto a piece of paper.

"Wade? What's going on? Is there a problem?"

Without turning around, Wade answered her, "Maybe, I came by to see if there was something in the barn that could have made your mutt ill."

"Posey? But... How did you know she was ill?"

"The vet called me, so I wanted to see if I could find a reason for her illness."

"I realize this is a little town, but why in the world would the vet call the sheriffs department about my dog?"

Standing up and folding the paper into little squares, he looked right at Rachael. "Since the reason she was ill was because she ingested marijuana."

"What? How...? And you think that she got it in the barn? How could she? No one has been here except you and me and."

"...and the drivers," he finished.

"... and the boys."

"There are lick marks beside it, and it doesn't look like powered sugar to me. It's probably drugs and it's my duty to find out who dropped it here."

Rachael looked stricken, and without saying another word, turned around and went out the door, too upset to stay. She knew she hadn't had any drugs in the barn, she had never even held any drugs in her hand, but Wade acted like maybe she was to blame. What would he think if he knew what happened last year? Dropping down on her glider, she leaned over as though she were ill. *Oh God! I need your help! What is happening? I wanted this to be good, a new life and now this, please don't let me get involved again. I just can't face being accused for a second time. How did You stand it? You were so innocent, and You just took every evil thing they said and did. Is that the answer? To say nothing and let God take care of me? Oh I need your peace, please Jesus help me.* Hearing Wade's car start up, she hurried inside the house and left the lights off. She couldn't face him again if he came by. As she leaned against the door, she realized that this might jeopardize her relationship with Wade. *Oh God what about Wade? What will this do to our relationship? What if he doesn't believe I had nothing to do with this? How can I witness to him if he thinks I'm involved in drugs? Surely, he must realize that is was probably the drivers that had drugs in the barn. Oh, please help me to trust You to work this out to glorify You.*

Picking up her Bible so she could read later in bed, she filled the whirlpool tub and tried to relax in the hot bath, and then slipped into bed, missing her little friendly puppy curled up next to her. Posey had started sleeping at the foot, but each night she had gotten closer to Rachael until she had chosen to sleep curled up next to her, on her own little quilt where she could get pats from time to time. Sighing, Rachael turned to the Psalms, knowing that she would get comfort and peace from God's Word.

♦ CHAPTER TEN ♦

Rachael spent the next morning at the cabin, sorting and unpacking boxes of books, arranging her special books on the shelves the way she wanted them. She unpacked her laptop and spent some time online trying to price some of the little things she bought at the flea market.

While she drove to the vet's office, Rachael had decided not to discuss them calling the sheriff's office. She knew they were just doing their duty, and anyone else would have done the same thing. Still, it bothered her, wondering if they thought she was doing drugs. Posey was glad to see her and was now sleeping in the chair by Rachael.

She spent the rest of the day 'puttering' as her Nana would have said, getting her house the way she wanted it. Before she slept, she prayed for Bobby, hoping he would keep his word and come to Sunday School tomorrow. She was so burdened for him, because she had seen first hand what drugs could do and she hoped he would turn his life around before he was as addicted as his friend Randy. As always she prayed for Wade before she drifted off to sleep, trusting God to keep him safe and open his eyes to his need of a Saviour.

Sunday was a gloomy, gray rainy spring day. She would rather have stayed home, hiding, but by the time she was ready to go, she was looking forward to the lesson from Revelation. She felt a little insecure going alone; Rose had called, saying she just wasn't up to going today. Rachael was thrilled to see Bobby parking his car in the side lot. He looked around and seemed relieved when she stepped out of the door where he could see her.

"Hey Miss Rachael!"

"Hey yourself Bobby, I'm so glad you came today. Let's go find your class and I'll introduce you to your teacher."

Paul Bosley was watching for them and greeted Bobby by name. "I've seen you around town Bobby and I know your mom. Grab a seat and we'll get started. Here's a Lesson Sheet so you can follow along. I like to print out the scriptures so everyone can have a copy." Smiling at Rachael, Paul led Bobby to a seat in the middle.

While sitting with Mary before church started, Rachael was pleased when Bobby came up and asked if it would be okay if he sat with some of the kids he knew from school? And would she mind if he went to lunch with them instead of getting pizza with her?

Nodding, she realized that Paul was trying to get the kids to include Bobby, and was thrilled to know that he would be meeting peers that would not be doing drugs and drinking and yet could still have a good time. She and Mary prayed for him before the service started.

Since Mary had to go to work after church let out, Rachael went to the fast food drive through and took her sandwich and salad home to share with Posey. The sun had come out a little and they sat on the glider sharing lunch and hugs. Posey was still a little subdued, but seemed to be recovering well. Rachael was upset that her little dog had been the recipient of someone's careless, selfish behavior. She had tried not to think about what happened last night with Wade, but realized that his job required him to check out the drugs in the barn. If she had to, she would tell him about Randy, but she really wanted to stay out of the problem with him.

Hearing a car slow down she glanced up just as Wade pulled into the parking spaces on the far side of the fence. By the time he had walked to the steps, Posey greeted him by sniffing his hand and then jumped back on the glider.

"How is she? Better?" Wade looked serious, but at least he was here. She wasn't sure if that was good or bad. Things were strained between them and she didn't know how to fix it.

"Yes, thank you, she's a little more inhibited than usual but that's not necessarily a bad thing. She's sleeping a lot and wants to be close."

"Rachael, we need to talk. I need to know how the drugs got into the barn. Do you know?"

"So you're here for your work?"

Wade nodded, and then impatiently blurted out. "Not just work! This is my work but we're friends and I don't want to hurt you but I need to do my job."

"Well Deputy Marsdon, I have no idea how the drugs got into the barn. I guess you know that they're drugs?" At his nod, she continued. "I can give you Mr. Anderson's number; he can tell you how to get in touch with the drivers."

"I already know who they are. I have their names and address, I checked them out the first time they were here. Do you know where they come from or where they called you from?"

"I don't know anything about them."

Wade looked hesitant, then determined. Sitting down on the bench across from her glider, he went on. "The night I came here to get my notebook, there were drugs in your waste basket. Do you know how they got there? I know no one had been here since I emptied the trash."

A tear rolled down her face, Rachael spoke softly, "And you think I am doing drugs? Why? I have never given you any reason to think that I was involved in anything illegal... Except, you're such a good sheriff, that I bet you've checked me out also? Read my records, file, or report or whatever you call it? And what did you find out Wade? That my brother is in prison for shooting my grandmother and that he was high on drugs and accused me of selling them? Is that why you can come here to my house and accuse me of something?" She was hurt to her soul, and wounded. Somewhere deep inside of her she recognized that it wouldn't hurt so much if she didn't care so much about Wade but she put that aside to think about later. Right now, she just wanted him to leave.

"I'm sorry, Rachael but finding drugs in your house and the barn means I have to ask hard questions. It's either me or Mitch."

Just then, a car pulled up beside the squad car, and Bobby jumped out, waving at them.

Rachael just had time to wipe her eyes before he was on the porch. "Hello Deputy Marsdon. Hey Miss Rachael! I wanted you to be the first to know! Mr. Paul and a bunch of us went to get pizza, and then he and I went to the park to talk. He explained all those things you talked about here the other day and answered my questions. Boy! He's so smart! He knows exactly where everything's found in the Bible, and showed me all the verses. It was exactly like you said the other day! God sent Jesus to pay for our sins so we could live forever with God in heaven. But right now, if we ask He'll come into our hearts and live so we can start being like Jesus. And I did it! I asked Jesus to be my Saviour, and prayed and told Him I wasn't good enough to be with Him, but was going to trust in Jesus to cover me. And oh, Miss Rachael I feel... so clean and loved! Mr. Paul said you can't go on feelings but have to rely on faith, and you have to trust Him everyday to take care of you like he promised." He was so excited; he hadn't realized that he was interrupting something serious.

Rachael hugged Bobby and held his face between her hands, "I'm so glad for you Bobby, the decision you made today will be the most important one you'll ever make in this life. Don't ever forget that God loves you and now you have a spiritual family that will stand by you. You may come to me anytime you have questions."

"Do you think you could talk to my Mom? She mentioned that you have invited her to church and left a paper on the table about being saved. She said she read it that night but didn't understand it. I read it over and over until I understood better, but going to Sunday School really made it clear. Mr. Paul's so cool! So you think you could talk to mom? She's worked so hard for me all her life, and the way I was going was just going to cause her hurt. Now, maybe with God's help and new friends I can help Mom better."

"Bobby, friends are very important, and now that you have a new responsibility, your old friends will probably make fun of you and tease you. Randy will still want you to drive him and do drugs. But don't let them talk you into anything that Jesus would not do. Don't think you can be with them and not act like them because you aren't strong enough yet."

Bobby shook his head. "Randy sure needs to change his life. He's really getting in deep. I'm glad you made him go home the other day." Glancing at Wade, he asked Rachael to pray for Randy.

"Oh Bobby, I've prayed for both of you boys since the first time I met you. And I still will. You're right, Randy's getting worse". Putting her hand on Bobby's knee, she asked. "Bobby will you tell me if Randy was smoking pot or drugs of some kind in the woods along the path? I found a butt that I picked up and put in the trash."

"Yeah, I told him not to, it was too close to the barn where everyone was working, but he wouldn't listen. Somehow, he had gotten some heavy stuff and wanted to try it. He dropped it when someone came out, and we left."

Wade, who was looking very miserable by now, wanted to know if Bobby knew where the drugs were coming from. "Son, the Sheriff and I are getting close to catching the drug runners here. If you're involved in any way, I suggest you back off completely or you'll find yourself in jail along with Randy. Someone's dropping drugs off by plane; do you know where the drop off location is?"

Bobby looked confused, but after getting a nod from Rachael, he confessed. "Maybe, I haven't ever done anything but pot, but Randy's into some bad stuff. One night he called and said he had a job making two hundred bucks and if I'd drive him to pick up something, he would give me fifty bucks. We drove up in the campground area, and after the plane dropped off a small package, we turned around and drove off. About fifty feet from the gate, a car pulled in front of us blocking the way and a scary guy in a mask got out carrying a shotgun. He motioned for the package and handed Randy the money. After that, Randy bought some hard stuff at the mall north of here. Man! I was scared, I told him I wouldn't do anything like that again, and he called me a wimp, but I'm not going to jail just to please him. I don't want to rat on my buddy, but the drugs scare me, Randy's changing, getting high all the time. If my telling can get him straight, then I guess it's okay. "

"Do you think you could find the drop spot on a map? How far was it?"

"I could try, it was dark, and I just followed his directions. I might be able to drive it better than look on a map. I guess I drove maybe twenty minutes or so."

"Do you have time to go now? I could take you and maybe we could find it together."

"I guess. Mom's working till seven. Mr. Paul's letting the teens play basketball tonight at the gym. I kinda wanted to do that. Say, Miss Rachael, the guys were really neat today! They included me in everything! I always thought they were snobs, but they aren't, they're really friendly."

♦♦♦♦♦♦♦♦

Rachael was glad to see them go. She was emotionally drained. The discussion with Wade had really shaken her, and then the excitement of Bobby being saved. She took just a moment to call Rose and Mary to share Bobby's news, asking them to pray for her as she talked to Donna tomorrow evening after work at the café.

Taking some aspirin for her headache, she spent a long time reading her Bible and praying. Wade had hurt her deeply, but on a rational level, she understood the reasoning for his questions. On a personal level, she felt like a failure for not being a better witness to him.

If he had seen Jesus in me, he wouldn't have doubted me at all. He would have trusted me. Here I am, owing him thousands of dollars for this house, and all my stuff in his barn. Lord? Help me to be patient and trust in You to work this all out.

She made a pot of tea and took Posey outside to the porch to watch the sun set. She was very discouraged and depressed. As she viewed the marvelous sunset, she realized that she needed to do what her friend Janice always told her, praise Him and t hank Him. By the time the sun was just a memory, she had decided to call her friend and have her pass the word to pray for the situation here and for Wade's salvation.

The next day she was in a better frame of mind, the talk with her friend had been just what she needed! She missed her so much. It was the one thing that had been negative about moving away to start a new life, she would be leaving friends she had known for many years, friends that prayed with her and shared her love of God. Janice had reminded her that we can't see the end result like God does; we just need to continue to trust Him. She also reminded her of Queen Esther and her Uncle Mordecai saying. 'and who knoweth whether thou art come to the kingdom for such a time as this?'

♦ CHAPTER ELEVEN ♦

Mary, whom she had found out was actually Marigold, much to her amusement, had given her directions to a large antique mall about forty minutes away, and so she spent the day, browsing around, just enjoying looking at all the displays, getting a feel for what the people in the area were selling. She had brought her expandable bags and by mid afternoon had filled them both up with things that caught her eye. She had come across a booth with a shelf of Christian books and had bought so many she had to take them to the car immediately. They had been a little high priced, but by buying so many the vendor had given her a discount. By the time she returned home she was tired but happy with her day. She freshened up and took a sandwich out onto the porch while Posey ran around the yard.

Bobby parked his car in the lane, and he and his mother walked up to the house. Posey ran around in circles and greeted them nicely. Donna looked tired; she had put in twelve hours today, on her feet, trying to serve demanding customers.

Rachael had prepared for the meeting; she had made some iced tea and had stopped by the bakery for some cookies. But more importantly, she had asked her Father to give her just the right words to reach Donna. She knew that Donna had raised Bobby by herself, working long hours and trying to make ends meet with little help from anyone else. She needed to know that God would be with her and she could lean on Him.

Donna seemed tense, so Rachael tried to put her at ease, asking her about her job and talking about Bobby. She handed Donna another tract and shared with her what Bobby had done and how she could have the same peace he has. When Donna admitted that she didn't understand; that just praying a prayer didn't seem like it was much, Rachael took her Bible and explained how God said to call on Him and He would answer. She was acknowledging that God is, and that He sent His Son to pay for our sins, so that we wouldn't be puppets, but come by our free will, asking Him to take control of our lives. She turned to the Bible verses that showed that God loved her and wanted her to trust Him and He promised, "Never to leave her or forsake her". Once she became His child, she could quit struggling and let Him take care of her.

Realizing that Donna did not understand yet, Rachael asked her to come to church Sunday and hear the Pastor explain more about what she had been telling her. He would also set apart time to counsel her, and help her make a decision.

Bobby had been quiet but now he interrupted, "Mom, please? This is important! Will you ask Stan to let you off Sunday so you can go with me? I want you there when I tell everyone what I did. You've worked seven days for years; surely you can take a morning off."

Seeing the earnestness in her son's face, Donna declared that Sunday would be a holiday for her; they would go to church and then somewhere other than the cafe for lunch! She also mentioned that Stan was thinking about selling the café, and she was concerned about her job.

During the next week, Mr. Anderson called wanting some furniture, so Rachael went to another flea market looking for things on his list. She had to pay more than she wanted to, but it was still in his limit. Saturday there was an auction/flea market at the fairgrounds that she had planned on attending; she thought maybe Mary would go with her if she wasn't working. Mr. Anderson was going to send the drivers by on Saturday night to get whatever she had in stock.

She had not seen or talked to Wade all week. She'd gone over to have lunch with Rose one day, and enjoyed the corn chowder and the friendship. She knew Rose was worried about Wade, and she probably knew something was strained between them, but if so she kept it to herself. Rachael knew Rose was praying for them. Everyone could tell her illness was wearing her out. She tired easily, and spent much time reading her Bible and praying for the ones on her list and for her friends. She seemed content, grateful for the time she still had.

Bobby came by one night, and said that Donna was still planning on going to church with him on Sunday and he was excited. He told Rachael that he had found the drop site for Wade, but had been asked not to talk about it. He offered to help move anything she needed, but instead of working, they just sat and watched the sun go down and talked about the changes that Bobby was facing. He wasn't daunted by his friends teasing; he already realized that he had something better than the drugs and booze.

Wade finally called on Friday, but all he wanted to know was if the drivers were coming any time soon to pick up a delivery. After telling him that they would be here on Saturday about eight PM, he asked if they knew where she lived.

"No, I told them I lived farther out of town, to call when they were fifteen minutes away and I would meet them here. I didn't think they needed to know I lived next door."

He agreed, saying "That was really smart, please don't mention this to anyone" and hung up. So much for being friends!

Friday she puttered around in the barn, trying to get an idea about arranging her furniture and small items so that they would draw in customers. While she was at the cabin fixing a sandwich for lunch, she heard a car drive up and looking out she saw Sheriff Stone.

After opening the door to him, he nodded and said, "Ma'am, I have a few questions to ask you? Do you have time?"

Offering him a sandwich, she fixed him a huge ham and cheese sandwich and a cup of fruit salad she had made, joining him at the table to share their lunch.

"I take it this is official business Sheriff?"

"Partly, I want to ask you about Randy. Rumor has it that he came over here to help you and you sent him away. Will you tell me why?"

As Rachael hesitated, he said, "I really need to know Rachael. I think this blasted drug dealer has got him hooked on drugs to get back at me for busting him previously. If Randy's involved in anything illegal, I need to get him protected."

"Bobby drove Randy here and when he came in the house, his eyes were glazed. When I confronted him, he wasn't totally coherent, so I told him he couldn't come into my house if he had been doing drugs. He said it was just a little pick me up but Bobby says Randy has gotten into some heavy stuff and is getting addicted. He's really worried about him and so am I. Bobby's refused to drive him anywhere to get drugs. I'm really sorry about this Sheriff, Randy's on a downhill path and if something isn't done he'll do something that will jeopardize his future."

"Like your brother?"

Startled, Rachael's eyes watered up, but she continued the conversation. "Adopted brother… no, my brother was never any good. He was mean spirited and hateful to everyone from the time he came to us. His mother had been taking drugs while she was pregnant with him and he had to overcome that as a baby. He was cruel as a youngster and it escalated as he aged. He knew the risks of starting drugs, but he found they would let him escape the anger and hatred he felt toward everyone. My parents were wonderful godly people and did everything they could for him; loving him and finding counseling, researching into his problems, but he would never listen. By the time he was fourteen he was stealing and buying drugs. When my parents died and we went to live with Nana, he tried to steal from us; he would take things from the shop to pawn for drugs. Finally, when he was eighteen, Nana refused him admittance to the house or shop. She paid the rent and utilities for a small apartment, but other than that she had no contact with him… He scared me… I was glad when he was arrested and put into prison. Maybe he can get some help there, but at least he's off the streets where he can't hurt anyone else. They ruled that Nana's death was not a direct result of the assault, but I think if he hadn't shot her, she'd still be alive." Wiping the tears off her face, she continued again, "Randy's headed the same way. I don't know why he's escaping into drugs, whether his mother's death or something else is making him angry, but he needs help."

The sheriff looked so dejected, slumped in his chair that Rachael hurt for him.

"I've been working long hours to forget my pain of losing his mother and in the process I haven't helped Randy to handle his. He probably thinks I spend more time working than being with him, but I do my job so he can have a better place to live.

I guess I need to get my priorities in line." Shaking his head, he changed the subject. "I need to know about you. Have you ever done any drugs? Have you ever sold drugs or knowingly made it possible for others to use you to buy or sell drugs?"

"No! Sheriff Stone, I have never, ever been involved with drugs except for the knowledge about my brother. Well, Wade said the cigarette butt I picked up was marijuana, but I didn't even know that. Russell accused me of selling, but it wasn't true."

The sheriff studied her a moment, then he continued to talk with her. "Okay then, Wade said you weren't involved, but I needed to decide for myself. I'm going to trust you. Wade's instincts are good and he swears you're not caught up in this even with all the indications that you're involved. I need your help Rachael. Bobby called Wade and told him that there was a drop tonight that Randy wanted him to drive him to. Bobby refused, both to drive or loan the car, and called Wade. I told Randy I wanted him to go with me tonight to the movies, so that he wouldn't be there. We're going to stake out the area where the drop is, and I don't want Randy any where near there. Now that this is an official case with the DEA involved, if Randy is involved in any way, he'll get jail time. Maybe that's what he needs, but I'm not willing to let him have a record, so I'm going to take him away and put him in a drug rehab in the city. He's underage; I can sign him in. Maybe it'll straighten him out before it's too late. If he's unafraid of being in public spaced out, then something needs to be done immediately."

"Then, one other thing, Rachael. When Wade questioned you the other night about the cigarette butt and the powder on the floor of the barn, he had more information that he couldn't discuss. But now again we need your help. Your Mr. Anderson is a drug dealer; we have proof he's shipping drugs in the furniture you buy for him. The drivers pick it up and then hide packages in the furniture and drive it to various destinations. So you see, it wasn't just a little evidence. Wade was sick thinking you were involved. And I have to defend him; he didn't really believe you were involved, but we have to follow every lead, and they were leading to you."

"Last week, he watched your drivers unload the furniture into the barn and put drugs in it and then load it into their van. We were able to follow it down the chain, and the DEA are handling it. But, we don't think the drop tonight is the same drop as your guys."

"The drugs in our county have been here for at least four years. This thing with Mr. Anderson is new; it's a drop off spot and dispersion for the East coast. He sent you down here as a cover to pick up and disperse drugs. As far as we can tell he has two other people buying furniture for him, and it's going to various dealers along the coast. If the drivers are coming tomorrow evening about eight o'clock there must be a pick up close by. Small planes aren't allowed to fly at night, so they need time to make the drop and get back home. We need for you to find out anything you can about where they drove from. When you meet them here, offer them a snack or drink, and ask if they're tired, have they been driving long? Anything you can get will be helpful. We'll have men watching the roads into our county, but if they slip by and pick up the drugs without us watching for the plane we won't have the men responsible and will have to wait for another drop, which means this batch will go on the streets. Going backwards up a chain is difficult at best. So, anything you can find out tactfully will be helpful. Just don't let them get suspicious. There'll be a man close by if you have any trouble. Be sure to leave the door open when you're in the barn with them and leave as soon as possible. If they try anything, scream, holler, shout and someone will be there immediately."

Rachael had been listening, with her thoughts playing across her face. She had felt compassion for Randy, and then telling the story of her brother brought grief again. Then came the gratefulness when she heard Wade believed in her. Finally, she was just devastated when she heard how Mr. Anderson had used her. "I can't believe I let him use me to deliver drugs! Do you think he is somehow responsible for getting my brother involved? He was associated with my grandmother for years. He bought furniture from her and had it picked up in a van just like he has with me."

The sheriff reached over and patted Rachael on the shoulder, "I don't know, maybe; we might find out later. I'm sorry Rachael, I know this is a lot to dump on you, but I think you can handle it. From what I see you have that 'whatever it is' that will get you through this. Don't talk about this to anyone, not Bobby or even Rose. By Sunday, things should be better. If we can determine where the plane that makes the drops is coming from then we can backtrack from there."

Trying to focus on what he was saying, all she could think of was that Wade believed in her and God would protect her. Looking at the Sheriff, she smiled, "That 'whatever it is', is Jesus. Bobby found Him and that's what Randy needs to get him straightened out. He can give his anger to God and He will turn it into peace."

Shaking his head, the Sheriff rose, and remarked, "I don't know about that. But I do think some people like you and the Gardening Club have something special. That's the nicest bunch of ladies in town. They are the first ones to help when there's a need. They all seem to be happy no matter what's going on. Maybe I need some of that to get me through this with Randy. I wish his mother were alive. He needs a woman in his life."

"Have you ever thought about remarrying?"

"Yes, I was interested in a woman a few years ago, but between her long hours and mine and our boys, there just wasn't any time to get to know each other better and somehow it just never came to anything. We've been friends all our lives, I guess we just need to keep it that way."

As Rachael watched him leave, she realized that in just those few minutes she had glimpsed into the real man. She had always thought he was the type A personality, friendly, outgoing, flirty, but just now she had seen the lonely, unhappy man. He had revealed a side of himself that many folks probably hadn't seen.

As she cleared away the lunch plates and glasses, she wondered if he had been talking about Donna? It would fit, the long hours, the boys; she could see where they would be compatible. It was a shame for two lonely adults not to even have the time to enjoy getting to know one another better. Maybe she could plan a picnic when all of this is over. Rose wasn't the only one who could be a matchmaker!

Walking back to the huge barn, Rachael noticed that the red bud trees were open and the bulbs were all blooming. Spring in the east was beautiful and she was thankful she was here. Deciding to open the double doors in front, she walked through the aisle between the boxes and stacks of merchandise. It was all she could do to get the doors open and propped up with the bars to hold them. After taking a few minutes to sit in the sun, she finally decided that she must, really must, get busy!

♦ CHAPTER TWELVE ♦

Her phone rang about eight that night, shattering the quiet. She had been praying for the men that were trying to catch the drug dealers tonight. They needed to find out where the plane was leaving from, and she prayed specifically for that. When the phone rang, she reached to answer it quickly.

"Hello Rachael, this is Laurel, Wade's out of reach for another hour, and his mother's had an accident. Can you go over to the house and see what's going on? The caregiver thinks she needs to go to the hospital, but doesn't want to take her without a family member knowing. Right now you're the closest thing to family."

"Of course, I'll go right away." Taking a minute to ask God for guidance, she changed into warmer clothing, picking up her purse and keys on the way out the door. Since she didn't know what she was getting into, she let Posey out and picked up her leash.

Deciding it would be better to have her along, than have to come home to let her out, she scooped her up and drove over to Roses house, parking away from the back door. The caregiver, a wonderful lady named Kate, met her at the door.

"Oh Miss Rachael, I'm so glad you've come! I was right there, and she opened the refrigerator door to get the butter and it swung closed on her and hit her arm. I could hear the bone crack. She's just so fragile! I put some ice on it and a bandage to keep the swelling down, but she wouldn't let me take her to the emergency room until I called Wade."

"Wade's not available for a while, so I came to see what I could do. That must have been so frightening for you both- I'm so glad you're here. Let's go talk to her."

Seeing Rose lying on her bed with her arm bandaged and raised, Rachael couldn't help but cry. Rose didn't need this on top of the cancer! But as soon as that thought came, she realized that it wasn't her place to judge. God was in control and He knew exactly what had happened, and He would give Rose the grace to go through whatever she needed to do.

Rose had taken a strong pain pill and even with that, she cried out when they moved her into the car. Kate wanted to take her own car, it was bigger and then she would have it available to go on home in. Rachael drove also, meeting them at the emergency entrance. She had called ahead, refusing an ambulance, but informing the staff that Rose was coming, and that she had already taken medication for pain. The staff was waiting with a wheel chair at the emergency doors, and took her immediately inside to be examined and X rayed.

After just a short time, Rose's doctor came out to find Rachael. They had met before and she really liked the gentle, kind, doctor. He had treated both Rose and Mr. Marsdon for years, and had attended the surprise birthday party for Rose.

"Hello, my dear. Rose does have a broken arm; we have gotten it aligned again and she's resting. It's swollen and with her cancer, I'm not sure how it will heal. We will just have to wait and see how it is when the swelling is down. I don't want to put a cast on it yet; a brace and a sling will work fine. This isn't unexpected, but won't do her any good. She's a wonderful lady though and we'll see her through this. Now, I want you to go home and rest! Tell Wade not to come till in the late morning, we won't know anything and she needs quiet. She will be fine in a day or so with pain meds. We might even let her go home for a few days with a sling until the swelling is down enough to cast it. The best thing you can do is pray, and I understand you can handle that!"

Rachael drove back to Rose's house, thinking she would leave a note for Wade, but then she decided that she would stay and talk to him herself. She found the afghan and curled up on the loveseat with Posey tucked in front of her.

Wade turned into the drive and was surprised to find Rachael's car parked there. He had not talked to anyone from the office and immediately he wondered if something had happened to his mother or maybe Rachael had been threatened. Quietly entering the kitchen, he turned the light on over the stove and could see Rachael on the loveseat with Posey. The little dog looked up, wagging her tail, hoping for some attention. Kneeling down beside Rachael, Wade gazed at her for a minute, hating to wake her but wondering what the problem was. Posey stretched and then licked Wade, bringing a grin to his face. The little ball of fur was really getting to him; she truly was adorable.

Finally, Wade touched Rachael on the arm and shook her a little; immediately her eyes opened and she smiled. "Oh Wade, you're home."

Leaning over Rachael, Wade was struck with the intimate setting and the closeness he felt with her. Gently he leaned down and kissed her lightly on the lips. It was all he could do to lean away and not focus on how much he enjoyed the intimacy.

"Well, sleeping beauty, is there a reason you're sleeping on our loveseat?"

Rachael hadn't moved. She was shocked that he had kissed her, it was the first time he had ever indicated that he cared for her. Oh, how she wanted to put her arms around him for another! With her thoughts in a whirl, she searched his face, and finding just a gentle look, she finally answered.

"Oh, yes, Wade, your mother broke her arm! We had to take her to the hospital. She'll be fine… they're keeping her until tomorrow. Laurel called me and I took her in to the emergency. I hope you're not angry that we didn't wait for you. You were needed there and I could handle this."

"No, of course not Rachael, thank you for caring about Mom so much. I just wish I'd been here though. This blasted case is taking all my time that I wanted to spend with Mom. I'm so sorry she's hurt. Do you think they would let me in to see her this late?"

"No… The Doctor said to tell you that you could come late morning. You need to get your sleep and then go. Your mother knows you love her. She's probably asleep by now anyhow; they gave her something else to let her rest. This isn't life threatening, she'll probably be home tomorrow."

Rachael had gotten up and had been fixing him a sandwich as they talked, and now she picked up her things and told Wade she would be gone tomorrow, but that she would check on his mother at dinner time. Calling Posey, who was sitting at Wade's feet begging for some of his sandwich, she turned towards the door.

"Wade? Did you do any good tonight?"

"Yes, I think we got the information we needed to stop this dealer. We'll know more in the morning when the DEA guys report back. We couldn't have done it without Bobby's help. He got us onto the drop site, and we were there waiting for them to fly past. The Drug guys got some night photos with their plane identification on it, and they were going to have agents at the airport when it landed. That will give us the men who fly the plane, and they can be traced back. In all, it was a good night's work. It's good when the men all work together to stop criminals. Sometimes there is a lot of competition between agencies but we all work for the same reason."

"I'm so glad; it's an answer to prayer. I hope it can be stopped soon."

♦♦♦♦♦♦♦

Saturday morning was absolutely the most wonderful spring day! The trees around the property were starting to bloom, and the grass was green. It had been cool enough that Rachael had to close her window before dawn, but the weatherman promised a high of seventy-one today! She dressed quickly and walked to the barn to pick up the furniture van. Mary had called to tell her she couldn't go to the flea market, she had a project to do, so she had called Bobby and he seemed excited to go and look around with her. She had promised if he would help carry and load the van that she would buy him whatever he wanted for lunch! Which turned out to be Pizza, of course! She had never seen anyone so hooked on pizza. He just loved it! The greasier the better!

They had a marvelous time! Bobby was funny and helpful, he flirted with the girls he knew, and carried bags. He was able to make the arrangements for the big furniture to be taken to the van, with out complaining or making negative remarks. In just a week, he had changed from a sullen, unhappy teen to a friendly happy, outgoing guy. She was thrilled to see the change in him and told him so. He grinned, "Everything's cool now. I've got a job for the summer helping at the church, doing the grass and whatever Mr. Paul wants me to do. I'll have time to help you move stuff around in the barn. But best of all, my Mom is coming to church tomorrow, and your buying me pizza for lunch, how good is that! Come on I'm starving!"

Driving home, Rachael realized that she was not worried about the drivers coming tonight. She was however, concerned about the safety of the law enforcement men. Right before they pulled into the drive leading to the back of the barn, Bobby suddenly spoke up. "Miss Rachael, can I tell you something?" After she assured him he could tell her anything and it wouldn't go any further, he shared with her what he knew about Randy. "He wanted me to go last night to pick up a package and I said 'no way dude', then he wanted my car, but I told him 'no way'; his license is restricted. I hated to do it, but I knew he'd get into trouble with the law and I didn't want him involved. So, I called Deputy Marsdon, and he must have told the sheriff. Anyhow... after school, the sheriff came to the pizza place and got Randy, saying he wanted to spend some time with him. Then Mom said he came in to the café about midnight and he looked really tired and depressed. His uniform had mud on it and he had some scratches on his face. There wasn't anyone in the cafe so Mom sat down with him and he told her he had put Randy into a rehab center in the city. She said he just hung his head and said 'I've really let him down, this is my entirely my fault. I should have spent more time with him and not out looking for other people's kids. But after I put the scumbag in prison for selling drugs in our county, I'm going to see that Randy is my priority.'"

"Oh Bobby, that's good news! The sheriff really loves Randy, and now he can help him. And also, maybe have some time for a personal life of his own. I hope they were able to do some good last night, I have been praying off and on all day."

"Me too! Wow! Can you believe it? God hears me when I pray? This being a Christian is awesome!"

That brought a laugh from Rachael, and as she parked the van she asked Bobby to help her unload later. "Can you come about seven thirty? I have something to do, and that would be a good time for me. It won't take long; we can have some donuts after."

The pathway through the woods to her house was getting pretty well trampled down, and the trees were shady. She wanted to put a little bench beside the huge sycamore tree so she could have a place to pray. As she came out of the trees, she was surprised to see cars parked in the parking area and along the road. As she grew nearer, she saw ladies everywhere! She slowed down and finally it came to her! It was the garden club, the 'Blooming Idiots'! They were planting her yard!

"Oh how wonderful!! Hello ladies, look at what you have done! Its' beautiful! Oh thank you so much." Rachael was thrilled to see a path with a glider and a tree for shade. There were plants in bricked off flowerbeds and rose bushes by the steps. It was all so pretty, and she was deeply touched. Hugging each of the ladies, she thanked them and looked at each area of the yard. Fern said each of the ladies had planted flowers representing their names so she would never forget them. As she went around the yard, they told her what they were and that some of them were underground and would appear at a later time. When she asked what the bushes were at each end of the cabin, Rhoda spoke up. "Those are mine, pink Rhododendron."

"Oh Rhoda I never connected your name!!! Rhododendron!! Really?"

"Well, actually it's legally Rhoda, but Mom told everyone it stood for Rhododendron. Thank goodness Mom didn't stick me with the whole thing!!!"

The ladies were almost finished, and Rachael offered them something to drink, but they had brought their own cooler and treats. They finished up their areas, and swept the walkway. Mary shared that even though she hadn't helped with the work, Rose was the one who had planned the layout and ordered the plants and walkways.

When Rachael thanked the ladies, offering to pay for the plants, Fern shook her head, "We want to thank you for moving to our community. We hope you'll stay a long time and enjoy living here. We'd love it if you'd consider joining our group, to help others enjoy the wonderful color of the plants and flowers that God has given to us. We think having flowers makes people happy. We'll be planting at the gazebo next week."

"I'd love to help you; it would be my pleasure, but you'll have to teach me about the flowers, I've never had a yard to take care of."

Posey was more than ready to go outside, she had been watching from her perch on the back of a chair, barking whenever anyone was close by. Now Rachael decided that she would take her out on the leash, in case the little rascal wanted to dig in the fresh dirt. That was certainly a good idea, she decided. Posey wanted to sniff at each new spot where the earth was freshly turned and planted. Rachael was patient though and soon the little dog realized that she could not bother the plants. Just a little tug on the leash let her know not to dig, and before long, Rachael took the leash off so Posey could run around 'sniffing and snooping'. She was pleased that she was so well behaved and could be loose and not try to dig up the plants.

♦ CHAPTER THIRTEEN ♦

Rachael made a quick trip to see Rose, and then headed home to get a bite to eat before she needed to be at the barn. Just as she finished her dinner, she heard Bobby's car along the road, so she picked up her cell phone and keys and went to meet him. When they arrived at the barn, she drove around to the back, parking facing out toward the street in case she needed to get away speedily. She parked so she wouldn't block the other van coming in, but would be close by if they needed to get out. She had not told Bobby about the driver's involvement with drugs; the sheriff had asked her not to. But she didn't think they were in any danger, she just wanted someone else with her.

They unloaded her purchases out of the van, storing them in the stalls. Then she took her polish and went over the new furniture, wanting it to look as good as possible. While Bobby meandered around the barn, she went into the office to do her paperwork, but as she pulled up her accounts, she realized that this might be the last shipment she would handle. If Mr. Anderson was involved in dealing drugs as they thought, she would be losing her job, and also the van. She might have to open her shop earlier than expected, and also purchase a utility van.

The drivers entered the barn through the back door and approached Rachael. Nodding at her, Buddy handed her a note from Mr. Anderson; he wanted an extra couple of pieces of furniture if she had them. Although they weren't exactly the same, she did have a couple of end tables she could send with him. He wanted ones with drawers underneath. She offered the men some drinks, but Buddy said, "Nah, we stopped awhile ago, we're good."

"Are the roads busy? Did you have a long drive?"

Sam volunteered, "Nope, we just had a couple hours. Lots of semi's though."

Nodding Rachael agreed. "The highway is always busy, is it bad coming south?"

Buddy gave her a quick look, but she had on a bored look and he decided she was just making small talk. "The road from here to the state line is full of semis at this time of day."

"I might need the van in the morning- what time are you leaving? I'll have to get the key."

"S'posed to be gone by six. Mr. Anderson wants this stuff right away."

Shaking her head, she grinned, "That's too early for me. Just leave the key on the counter please."

Rachael didn't think she would learn anything else, so she told them she'd show them where the end tables were and they could get the rest off the van.

Bobby had been wandering around, they had seen him when they entered, then he had slipped out the door while they talked. Now he walked over to the van, and after checking to see if he was being watched, he glanced inside, then stood on the step and reached into the right side seat. Then he whistled and soon heard a noise in the woods. Being sure no one followed him, he carefully walked toward the sound. Just as he entered the woods, a hand grabbed him around the shoulder and one covered his mouth.

As soon as he calmed down and saw it was the Sheriff, he nodded, and then whispered to him. "Those guys are creepy. The big dude is high and the other one is carrying a knife in his belt. I picked up this map off the floor of the cab, there's a package on the floor also and a fifth of whiskey on the seat. The keys are in the ignition. There's a shot gun lying between the seats. I'm going back and get Miss Rachael."

The sheriff was looking at the map Bobby had handed him and found one marking on it. Showing it to Bobby, he asked if he knew where it was. "Gosh, yes, let me get Miss Rachael out of there and I'll tell you."

"Good job, Bobby, be careful. Put this back in as you go by. Wade'll meet you at Rachael's; tell him what you know and then I want you to go straight home, and don't talk about this."

Rachael was thankful when Bobby entered the barn again, and they could leave. When she turned into her driveway, Rachael was relieved to see Wade's truck parked beside Bobby's. They found him on the glider, with Posey on his lap.

When they entered the cabin, Bobby told him what he had found, and Rachael shared what little she knew. Then Bobby told Wade that when he had taken Randy to a party north of here, the kids had gotten really high and were doing stuff that even then he didn't want to do, so he left. As he came out onto the road leading to the campground, a green truck had come past with two guys in it, and they might be the drivers. The spot marked on the map was close to the shelter in the far corner of the area.

Wade confirmed that Buddy had a green truck without a tailgate; he had driven it here the first time they brought the van. Since Bobby could show Wade where it was, Wade thought they could find the drop off. Turning to Rachael he put his hand on her shoulder.

"You've both done really well. We're getting close to catching the main distributors. Now I want both of you to stay home and not talk about this to anyone else. Rachael, don't go to the barn until you know they've left in the morning. We have men protecting you, but don't put yourself in jeopardy. Bobby, take off, but be careful. Thanks again for your help."

As Rachael was getting ready for bed, she went over in her mind all that had happened, realizing that even though Wade had talked to her, she didn't know if he totally trusted her yet. He had been very professional, of course, talking about the situation with the drug dealers. She had been so glad to see him, she worried about his safety, but that didn't mean she could let him know how she felt.

Sitting in her pew the next morning, thinking about the Sunday School lesson, she was shocked when she heard Wade's voice ask her if there was room for him! She turned and saw him standing next to his mothers' wheelchair. Lowering her eyes to Rose who was smiling, she scooted over saying, "There's always room for you Wade."

Her thoughts were going round and round! How had Rose been able to be out so soon? And how had she talked Wade into coming with her? She had so many questions, but tried to listen to the Pastor. Wade seemed relaxed next to her as they shared a hymnbook and then during the message from the Pastor, he sat quietly, not fidgeting. Rachael was not relaxed! She was very aware of Wade, knowing her feelings were getting stronger all the time. She had finally had to face the fact last week that she was really drawn to him emotionally, and knew that before long she wouldn't be able to deny that she was in love with him.

After church was over, Wade excused them from lunch, saying his Mother had promised to rest all afternoon if he brought her to church. That left Rachael alone for lunch again, so she shared with Posey and played ball in the yard with her. There hadn't been any time to talk to Rose, since Wade wanted her to rest, but he had mentioned that he wanted to stay home with her today.

Thank you Lord, whatever it takes for him to understand how much You love him. Touch him and open his heart to Your Word. You have promised that Your Word will never return void, that there is always a result to hearing Your Word. Please make Yourself real to him. Thank you, in Jesus name, Amen.

When she returned home from the Sunday evening Bible study, she was surprised to see Wade's car in the parking spot. He was sitting on the steps playing with Posey, throwing the ball and giving pats and encouragement when she brought it back. When Rachael sat down beside him, Posey didn't even stop running. Smiling, Rachael remarked to Wade, "So much for not liking my little friend. I think she likes you better than she does me."

"It's the uniform, it gets them every time."

"Hungry? Thirsty?"

"No thanks, I need to talk to you." He turned and leaned against the rail post.

He was fidgeting, holding Posey. "I just don't know where to start. This has been a hectic month; I have never been so confused in all my life."

He looked down and continued to stroke the little dog, but was quiet for a while. Rachael stayed quiet also, she knew he was struggling and needed time to sort out what was bothering him.

Finally, he looked up. "First of all Rachael I want to tell you that your coming here has greatly impacted this community. Because of you, we've gotten two drug organizations stopped in this county. Your helping Bobby allowed him to tell us where the drops would be. He would never have done that if it weren't for you. I can see a change in him already. Randy is getting the help he needs and we were able to keep him out of the situation. I'm sorry you lost your job, but if you can't start your business soon, maybe you can find something in town."

"Did you catch the guys last night?"

"The DEA had a man in a tree taking pictures when the plane dropped off the drugs for Buddy and Sam. They were able to get the number and are backtracking it, just like they did the first one. It won't be long before they close the whole operation down. You may have to have one more pick up, Mitch will let you know about that."

He paused, and then continued. "You're an amazing lady Rachael; I really wish I could tell you how much influence you've had on people. Mitch is much more respectful at work; everyone has noticed his attitude toward the ladies has been much better. Bobby thinks you're wonderful, (so do I by the way)! Mom loves you; she misses having you stay at the house. We talked today for a couple of hours. I understand a lot more now and I'm considering taking a leave of absence for a little while to spend time with her. I also want to keep going to church and read the Bible you left for me. You know, I started reading it the first night, and I have read John every day since. Over and over and over until finally I can say that I believe there is a God; that Jesus is His Son. I've also read the rest of the New Testament. I'm beginning to understand how much He loves us and wants us to be a part of Him. You remember when you said I needed to go with my heart, not just my head? Well, I didn't understand until Mom broke her arm. When you told me she had, I heard it; and was sorry. But when I saw her, then I felt it. My heart hurt for her. It made me realize I had been reading for understanding, and so I read again with belief. I wanted to know how it related to me. I still haven't sorted it all out, but I know I'm finally on the right path. I have an appointment with the Pastor tomorrow to see if he can answer the rest of my questions."

He stopped again, and Rachael sensed that the hardest part was still to come. It was all she could do not to interrupt him.

Reaching over to take her hand, he pulled her up to sit beside him on the glider, speaking quietly. "Rachael, I'm so sorry I didn't trust you. Please forgive me? Even in that, I trusted my head knowledge and not my heart. I had already read your record and knew about Russell and your grandmother. I also knew that he had accused you at the trial of selling drugs. Then when I found the drugs in the wastebasket and in the barn, I put that with the fact that Mr. Anderson and Buddy and Sam were involved in distributing a huge amount of drugs, it just seemed too coincidental. It's my job! This was the first time my personal life ever intertwined with my work and it really confused me."

"The more I was around you the more I felt that you could never do anything against the law. You've shown genuine Christianity over and over with everyone you came in contact with. In hindsight, I think you would say that God sent you here to bring all this out in the open and get it stopped. If that's true, it's because God can trust you to always put Him first. I've had such a struggle with all this, talking with Mom today she seemed to think it's God drawing me and opening my eyes to Him. I never thought I needed God in my life, but after you came, I found out that there was something missing. I've had to guard my emotions from my job, and I think I also shut everyone else out. I've found an empty spot that I think

God wants to fill; I need to decide where I stand on all of this and make a decision soon."

Shifting around so that he faced her more, he put his arm on the back of the swing. "I also found an empty spot in my heart for you. You are the most amazing woman! I have fallen in love with you; I can't imagine my life with out you." Seeing a sweet smile on her face, he wiped the happy tears from her eyes, and continued. "You know, I was jealous of Posey? I love seeing you in the cabin, you've made it a home and I like being here with you. You were right, it needed love and you have that. I envied the hugs and attention you gave to this little mutt. Do you have enough to include me?"

"I already have, Wade, I realized weeks ago, how important you are to me. I was just waiting for you realize how much God loves you." Looking into each others eyes, they could see the love they shared, and knew that the feelings were mutual.

After a sweet hug and kiss Wade murmured, "The other thing I wanted to discuss with you about is Mom. When I picked her up yesterday the Doc said that she probably won't be able to get out much in a few months. Do you think you might forgive me by then and agree to marry me? I know it's soon, but I do love you, you know. Even when I tried to stay away because of work, I realized that my feelings for you. You, my sweet, are a detriment to logical thinking. Besides, you have to marry me; Mom started planning our wedding the first day we talked in the café. She hopes for a June wedding when the flowers are blooming. The 'Blooming Idiots' have all the flower arrangements already planned!"

Searching his face, Rachael could see the love she was looking for, and she gently leaned forward and kissed him. "I love you too, and I'll marry you in June with only one condition."

"Just one's not bad… maybe."

"I would like to name our first daughter after my mother and yours."

"Hmm, I don't know your mothers name, is this something that's really going to be as bad as 'Posey'?"

"It will be beautiful; Heather Rose Marsdon!"

"You're kidding! Your mother was named after a flower?"

"Yes, I knew the night of the garden club party that God had sent me to a place where I would fit in and be loved. When I finally admitted to myself that I was falling in love with you and thought about a future together, I realized that we would have the perfect name for a daughter."

Holding her close, Wade whispered, "It's a perfect name. So… Does this mean we are engaged? I want you to be Mrs. Wade Marsdon."

"Hmm, that sounds good too. I think your mother will be thrilled, but not too surprised. She's been praying for us since the very first day."

"I know, she told me. Well, that's okay; she loves us, and wants us to be happy. She told me today I need to be a good husband."

"Oh Wade, I had my Nana, but there was never a man in my life. I may not make a very good wife because I'm used to doing things by myself."

"Well, I've never been a husband, but I think between the two of us and Mom, and God we can have a great life! What do you think about living here in the cabin for a while, until we outgrow it, and using the house for a bed and breakfast? We'll have to stay there at first, to be with Mom, but later, after she's gone, I'd like to be here together for awhile."

"What a wonderful idea! Do you think we can handle that? It would take a lot of time to manage a B & B."

"Well, as the next Sheriff…! I think I can pretty much decide my own hours, and I was thinking about hiring someone to run it. The town needs another hotel."

"Wade! You're going to be Sheriff? What about Mitch?"

"Mitch is moving up also. He wants to work with the DEA. This thing with Randy has him really hyped up and he wants to get it stopped! He's planning to resign and that will put me in until the elections. The other guys don't want to be top man, they're happy just following orders, so I think I can plan on getting it permanently."

"I'm really proud of you! I think what you're doing is tremendous! Your mother will be so pleased. And I know just the person to run the B & B! Can you guess?"

"Well, you don't really know too many people yet, but I can't think of anyone. So, tell me, Mrs. Wade Marsdon to be, mother to be of Heather Rose Marsdon, who you have chosen?"

"Donna! She'll be perfect. That will give her a better home for Bobby. Even though she'd still be working, she'd be there all the time for Bobby. She would be there when he comes home from school."

"I don't know if Donna would be my first choice, she isn't the sweetest person in the world, she just might run off the customers before they check in."

"Just give her a couple of weeks! Jesus is going to fill her heart with love and she'll be a different person! She's tired now, with rest and a less stressful job, she'll just blossom! And if my hunch is correct you may be asked to be best man at her wedding before the year is out."

"What? Who's she seeing? I didn't know anyone was interested in her?"

"Just wait and see! Your mother is not the only matchmaker; I've been praying for some people and it's fun to see God work."

By now, Rachael was snuggled up on the glider with Wade, holding a sleeping Posey on her lap. As Wade leaned down to kiss her, she murmured, "Someday I'll tell you what I prayed for you!"